A SEVERE CASE OF DANDRUFF

D1809189

A Severe Case of Dandruff

Herbert Williams

with a preface by
Alun Richards

First Impression—1999

ISBN 1 85902 773 3

© Herbert Williams

Herbert Williams has asserted his right under the Copyright, Designs and Patent Act, 1988, to be identified as Author of this Work.

All rights reserved. No part of this book may be reproduced, stored in a retrieval system, or transmitted in any form or by any means, electronic, electrostatic, magnetic tape, mechanical, photocopying, recording or otherwise, without permission in writing from the publishers, Gomer Press, Llandysul, Ceredigion, Wales.

This book is published with the support
of the Arts Council of Wales.

Printed in Wales at
Gomer Press, Llandysul, Ceredigion SA44 4QL

For Dorothy

Preface

The long short story is one of the most rewarding forms of literature. Its pleasures are intense for it can be read at a sitting and, as a reader, your involvement is total. Undisturbed, you enter a world and for a while, if the author knows what he or she is talking about, you are held hostage, hearing and seeing with the eyes of another. Cyril Connolly once said that the abandonment of the form in England was solely due to the animosity of publishers. My view is that their accountants did not like slim books so Gomer Press are to be congratulated on breaking the mould. Herbert Williams' story is also, one suspects, autobiographical which makes it the more telling. To say that it is a sharply observed tale of a very young man's experience of a T.B. sanatorium is somehow to lessen its impact, for the world of the sanatorium and the terrors which the very letters T.B. induced when we were young is akin to the reaction to AIDS now. As they used to say in my sanatorium; once diagnosed, you were a strong candidate for an early fitting of 'the wooden suit'.

This feeling was widespread. It was not just that almost everyone knew someone who had died of consumption —itself an evil word—but that the healthy could be infected with apparent ease. Somewhere at the back of my mind is a never-to-be-forgotten statistic: an analysis of casual sputum deposits in a Monmouthshire mining valley park in the 1920s revealed that sixty-five per cent were still tubercular. Moreover, if you had someone in your family who had died of the disease, you were immediately thought to be vulnerable. In every school, college, factory or recruiting office, there was always someone asked to step aside for a mass X-ray. A shadow on the lung might be as insignificant as dandruff; or it might not.

Once diagnosed, the sanatorium was the next step, often after a long wait to obtain a bed. Once admitted you entered a regime. You were either on strict bed rest, as Herbert Williams describes it, 'a squalid regime of bedpan and urine bottle and blanket baths,' or you were allowed to get up to visit the lavatory, perhaps even the luxury of a shave when standing up. If you had cavities in your lung, you might be required to lie in a plaster cast on one side for month after month. You could not kiss anyone on the mouth and a telephone had to be disinfected after you had used it. Visitors were allowed between 3 p.m. and 5 p.m. on Saturdays and Sundays. If you had them at any other time, you were dying.

Worst of all were the voices of unreason exclusively belonging to the other patients. In my case, I had knocked about the world and a long experience of ships and barracks had prepared me for the all male wards where you could spend years if you did not respond to treatment. In Herbert Williams' tale, sixteen-year-old Ralph begins his treatment with a memory of a brother dead from the same complaint and a gentle, loving Aberystwyth home behind him. The shock of contact with the other world is therefore all the more painful, especially the brow-beating by the other patients, the constant, unremitting foul language, the close encounters with psychopaths, neurotics, saints and sinners, and worst of all, the old chronic patients whose highly suspect medical knowledge often became gospel as busy doctors skimped explanations. Resection surgery, thoracoplasties, all operations were meat and drink to the chronics, as I can testify. I hear one voice still.

'When I had it before the war, they done the operation under local anaesthetic and you could hear your ribs dropping into the bucket under the table one by one!'

Through it all, confined to your bed in chilling cold in the winter, the windows forever open, there were also your thoughts and worry itself, 'a demon burrowing into the back of the scalp, a hot, crawling nastiness poisoning everything'. You would see strong men visibly reduced in weeks and eyes made savage by despair. I once seized two Swan Vestas matchboxes full of illegally hoarded soneryl tablets from a would-be suicide and fought him off while I flushed them down the toilet. The process exhausted the two of us.

There is also, of course, recovery, the blessed days of first footsteps, the flakes of skin showering from the soles of feet long unused, an end to the democracy of pyjamas and a new entry into the social order of those allowed to take exercise in their own clothes. Young Ralph goes one better and meets a local girl outside the sanatorium on high days and holidays. His escape beginning, he grows reckless and even dares to kiss her *on the mouth*!

This is a story that should be compulsory reading by those who have never been really ill. It evokes a world that is long gone and made so by the discoveries of various chemotherapies, successful surgery and, in most of Europe at least, significant changes in living conditions and general health. It is also a tender evocation of a restricted adolescence written by a poet with a poet's sensitivity. And for those of us who have been down the same road, it is a timely reminder of our mutual good luck.

Alun Richards

Prologue

From a distance, it might have been mistaken for an open prison. The wooden huts were geometrically placed in long parallel rows. A tall central stack blew out smoke that curled and twirled in the clear mountain air. A small church in the grounds spoke of the consolations of religion. And men were at work there, digging and hoeing and weeding, cutting grass, sweeping leaves, according to the season.

But why were the cell windows flung open wide to all weathers? And why were so many of the captives lying in bed all day, or trooping the corridors in pyjamas and dressing-gowns? What manner of prison was this?

Few of them ventured down the long, curving drive to the unguarded gates. Why scorn a freedom so easily attained? What invisible obstacle held them back?

Only those who had endured there knew the answers. None of them forgot the place, but some—like Ralph—remembered more sharply than others.

'It was so long ago, wasn't it?' somebody once remarked.

'No,' he replied. 'It was yesterday.'

1 Initiation

'How long did they say you'd be in here for?'

Mel, frizzy-black-haired, looked across at the youth, shameless malice in his small brown eyes.

'Six months.'

'That's what they tell every fucker,' Mel gloated. 'Only dandruff cases get out in six months. You'll be lucky if you're out in two years.'

Ralph stared back. It was not so much the words that shocked him as the cruelty behind them. He was not used to people like Mel. He was used to people being kind to him. He was sixteen years and two months, and had been in the sanatorium for an hour.

Mel took the headphones from a hook beside his bed and slid under the bedclothes to listen. Jim, in the bed opposite, seemed dreamily unaware of the exchange.

'Don't listen to him,' said John. 'You may be one of the lucky ones.'

'Hope so,' said Ralph. But he knew he wouldn't be.

Four of them, Mel, Jim, John and Ralph, in Ward 8 of Block M in the shutaway world of the sanatorium.

'Chopin had the bug.'

'And Schubert.'

'Beethoven had it as well.'

'No he didn't, you daft cunt. He went blind.'

'That was Handel. Beethoven went deaf.'

'He went blind, I tell you.'

'He went fucking deaf.'

'He went fucking deaf *and* blind.'

13

Everything was fucking, everyone a cunt in defiance of gender. Fucking cunt, daft bugger, stupid bastard with a short, explosive 'a' or just plain shithead.

Ralph was not used to such talk. In every way he was a virgin.

'How are you feeling in yourself?'

Doctor John on his rounds. Shy, diffident farmer's son from West Wales, always the same question, never a breath out of place. Beside him Sister O'Neill, slim, fair, quick-blushing, bold tits mocking the frenzied dreams of the inmates. He stopped by every bed and she handed him a file. He glanced at it, smiled obscurely, asked his meaningless question and handed it back.

As they went on their way she pressed the files hard against her tits, as if fearing they might drop off.

The files were Top Secret. Case histories were only for doctors. 'The boys'—collectively they were all boys, whatever their ages—must not ask awkward questions. Theirs was to obey, for to disobey was death.

Ralph would obey. He wanted to get better and go home.

Bobby had gone home, but only to die. He had lasted eighteen months, sitting up in bed to play the recorder, playing 78s on the wind-up gramophone with best-quality steel needles, spitting neatly and dutifully into his hygienic blue bottle. He had his own knife and fork and spoon, tied round with cotton to identify them clearly.

He had died one Tuesday afternoon at a quarter to two. The house had smelt of flowers for ages.

Mel was singing. Lying against propped-up pillows, headphones clasped over frizzy black hair, absorbed. Listening to Welsh Rarebit on the wireless. A male voice choir.

Ralph hated Welsh Rarebit. He hated male voice choirs. He liked New Orleans jazz. Mel hated jazz of any kind.

Jim had the same taste in music as Mel. They were pals, more or less the same age. Ralph, at sixteen, was the youngest in the ward, John two years older. They had gone to the same school, but hadn't known each other well. The only clear memory Ralph had of John at school was of him sliding helter-skelter down the banisters from the chem lab, legs splayed out, laughing.

John was very ill now; Ralph feared he might die.

Cheerful, impish Sam Mitchell. Ralph's age, or perhaps a year older. Smooth-black-haired, a hell of a lad. Organising a football match, to be played in their dressing-gowns.

'Don't be daft, mun! It's not worth it.'

'You'll be mopping, I tell you.'

'They'll bloody see you. They'll throw you out.'

'Piss off. You're shit scared, the lot of you.'

Brave, defiant Sam Mitchell. Sister O'Neill got wind of it. She had a quiet word with him. The match was abandoned before it even began.

Mopping and staining were both bloody words. Mopping was the most dreaded symptom of all, a full-scale lung haemorrhage. Staining simply meant finding traces of blood in one's spit.

15

Blood, in the San, meant not life but death.

Tarzan was even madder than Sam. He was on Block G, where the younger patients went when they were getting better. It was further down the hill from Block M, near the curving drive that led to the gates and the big world beyond.

His old pals on Block M were proud of him. He was a hero of the war against the bug, a comrade who despised the enemy so much that he simply pretended it wasn't there.

'He was up on the fucking roof.'

'Swinging like a monkey.'

'He'll be chucked out if he's not careful. Jock won't stand for it.'

'He's not scared of bastard Jock.'

Jock was Mr Big, the Medical Superintendent. He struck fear even into the brave and had more power than a prison governor. No governor, however sadistic, can incarcerate someone indefinitely. But you were in the San as long as Jock wanted you to be; or were cast out for indiscipline, to fight the bug alone.

Every Monday morning those on graded exercise, like Tarzan, were summoned before Jock, who flicked through their files and determined their destinies. Some stayed as they were, on the same grade as before; others were promoted, some put back a grade. And there were those who, pitifully, were sentenced to a further period of bed-rest. Strong men had been known to weep after seeing Jock.

'He's a bastard.'

'He'd make Hitler look like Florence Nightingale, mun.'

'I reckon he's a sadist.'

And the most damning indictment of all. 'That man's a fucking Tory.'

At Jock's side stood Sister McGaw, a brooding presence in the San, a woman with a Dracula gift for inspiring fear. It was not so much what she said or did as the way she looked; square, grim, stolid, an avenging angel. Coldly she confirmed Jock's decisions with a bleak stare or inscrutable smile. She was the very spirit of the San; rigorous, inhuman, a penal institution for the diseased.

Haddock for breakfast every Monday: a tidal smell swamping up from the kitchen, just below Block M. Ralph, who often felt sick at the sight of food, could not face the pungent yellow horror.

'Get it down you, mun. It'll put lead in your pencil.'

'Don't know what's good for him. Fucking Aberystwyth cunt.' Not unpleasantly said; Mel's South-Wales-miner badinage.

John to his rescue. 'I don't blame him not eating it. I couldn't either.'

'You're another fucking Aberystwyth cunt, that's why.'

'The smell's enough to put you off.'

John, fastidious, avoided haddock by being on Absolute. He had steamed fish instead; Absolute Rest had its paltry compensations.

Ralph put his tray at the bottom of the bed and slipped down between the sheets.

'What's up, Ralph? Off your food today?'

Ted the orderly, collecting the dirty dishes. Ted was kind; he liked Ted. There were lots of people he liked. They made the future endurable.

By now he knew he was no dandruff case.

'Breathe in. Cough.'

Doctor John, targeting the stethoscope on various parts of his chest, listening intently to the furrowings of the bug.

Regular examinations. Regular X-rays.

Going for an X-ray meant the novelty of getting dressed and walking along the covered ways to Hospital Block. This was the domain of Dr Kerrigan: another Scot. Cast in the same iron mould as Sister McGaw, she managed a thin smile every Christmas.

Did she make Hospital Block, or did Hospital Block make her? It was a place where people went when death could be seen, beckoning.

Ralph dreaded going to Hospital Block.

'I'm not sure they're doing the right thing at all.' Ben Gulliver, smooth, clever, standing in his dressing-gown with his back to the radiator in Ward 8. Talking politics. 'After all, look what happened to the Groundnuts Scheme.'

'I don't give a monkey's about the groundnuts,' said Mel. 'They're right about this. Sting the fucking rich, that's what I say.'

'But if there are no rich left to sting,' said Ben, brow puckered, 'what then?'

'Exactly!' said John eagerly. 'That's what I've been

saying. But these—' He coughed; phlegm churned up from his lungs.

'There'll always be fucking rich,' said Mel. 'Get what you can from the buggers, I say.'

'There must be a limit, though,' said Ben carefully. 'You can't go on and on taxing the same people to the hilt.'

'Why not?'

'Because you'll tax them out of existence.'

'That'll be the day! Bugger me. That'll be the fucking day.'

Mel, swinging his sponge-bag, went to the dubs whistling.

Ben returned to his own ward. John sank back on his pillows.

'Any betsssss?'

Packer, skiving off from the grades, stood in the flung-open french window, small, tidy, detached. The sibilant was long-drawn-out and sly, a bookie's runner of a letter.

Mel had an accumulator, Jim a simple each-way.

Packer took their bets and moved on. John was asleep.

'Why'd they call him Packer?' ventured Ralph.

'Because it's his name, you daft cunt,' said Mel.

His temperature soared.

'How are you now then?' asked Sister Roberts, squinting at the thermometer.

'Not too good. I feel all washed up.'

'All washed up, eh?' Something about the phrase amused her. 'Can't have that, can we?'

She looked down at him kindly.

He liked Sister Roberts; small, darkskinned, pretty. Nice.

He couldn't set foot out of bed at all now, not even to go to the dubs. He was condemned to the squalid regime of bedpan and urine bottle and blanket baths; an awkward, embarrassing business.

There was an etiquette he quickly learned: you peed in the bottle first before sitting on the bedpan.

The screen pulled around his bed reminded him of the screens around the dead.

The orderlies took away the bedpans, grumbling.

He couldn't sleep. The night nurse swished along the corridor now and then, flashing her torch. Checking up. He shut his eyes, feigning sleep. As he lay awake, he thought about school and friends and football. He'd love to see Aber play again. He imagined a football match, kick-off and tackles, passes to the wing and tricky inside-forward dribbling.

He imagined Eddie Ellis scoring the winning goal and holding the Cup aloft.

He was all imagination.

They gave him tiny green sleeping pills which sent him off but made him wake up feeling awful. He was tired to the bone though in bed all the time and felt sick in his stomach.

'Get a porringer, quick!'

He vomited into the white china bowl.

Dear Ralph, wrote Billy,

I hope you're feeling better. It's funny without you

round here. Trefechan beat Penparcau 3-1 last Saturday. Georgie Christopher got two of the goals. I played for the Reserves a couple of weeks back. I didn't score but I made the first goal. I hope they'll pick me again some time. School's as bad as ever. I'll be leaving as soon as I can. Dad's getting me an apprenticeship as a plumber. I can't wait.

Mrs Phillimore died last week. She was so fat they couldn't get her in the coffin. They're pulling down the dosshouse. About time too. I saw Betty Pratt and she was asking after you. In fact she sent her *love*. Honest.

I hope you'll be home soon anyway so cheerio for now.

Your old pal,
Billy

Billy was Fit. Aubrey was Fit. Hughie was Fit. Even Teddy Edwards was Fit and you could hold him up to the light and see through him.

The world was divided between the Fit and the Dead.

They were dead to the world in the San. It was somewhere apart.

School was another century. So were friends. So was feeling normal.

He'd been ill for years, on and off. Feeling ill at breakfast. Forcing himself. Chomping and chewing. Trying to swallow.

Going to school feeling awful, his father walking beside him.

'You're not worried about Bobby, are you?'

'No.'

'We're doing our best for him. You know that, don't you?'

'Yes.'

'You mustn't worry about Bobby. He'll be alright.'

'OK.'

But he knew his father had been kidding him about Bobby.

Visitors. Between three and five every Saturday and Sunday. If you had them any other time you were dying.

Visitors. Creatures from another planet.

Sitting on chairs around the beds. Gassing. Being Cheerful.

'We'll soon have you out of here, boy, you watch!'

'Look better today, Jack. Bit of colour in your cheeks.'

'Duw, lovely view from here, mun. Worth a tonic just looking at it.'

'Don't they ever close them bloody windows?'

When the words ran dry they shuffled, coughed, squinted slyly at watches. 'Well well, that's it then . . . What can I be bringing you next time then?'

When they'd gone the silence took over. Mel put his dressing-gown on and went down the dubs for a pee.

Jim put on his headphones and slid down in the bed.

John turned on his side and slept.

Ralph thought of the football match he'd just missed on Town Field.

Sometimes his mother came, but not very often. It was too far, five hours by train and very expensive.

She stayed at Cherry Farm, with nice Mrs Phillips. Ralph had stayed there too, coming with Mam to see his eldest brother Joe when *he* had been a patient. Having the bug was a kind of family tradition.

'You alright, son?'

She sat beside his bed, rosy-cheeked, plump, grey hair tied neatly in a bun above her scrubbed neck. Smiling. Kind.

'Yes, I'm OK.'

'Got everything you want? Enough to read?'

'Yes, fine.'

Mam looked cheerfully around. She saw goodness everywhere. She saw, not Mel, but a frizzy-black-haired friendly man who was nice to her boy. Everyone was nice to her boy. Everyone was *nice*.

'Feeling better then, yes? Having a nice rest here?'

She embarrassed him. He was ashamed of his embarrassment.

He was sixteen and too old to have a mother.

Olive Chips, walking sprightly to work in the kitchen. Pert, dark, bosomy, fifteen and ripe for it. Walking to work along the covered way downhill from Block M. Looking up at him. Smiling.

'Go on, mun. Give her a wave!'

'Give her six inches you mean.'

'Ralph wouldn't know what to do with it, would you Ralph?'

'He'd say he'd seen a butcher's shop on fire!'

'Christ, Ralph, what's up with you? Give her a wave, mun!'

Olive Chips disappeared into the kitchen.

'Well, you stupid cunt. Missed your chance again.'

'Christ, I've got a hard-on. Wish that bint was up here.'

'Wish any fucking bint was up here.'

Every woman was a bint or a tart. Except girlfriends, daughters, mothers, wives. They were different. Bints and tarts were just for stuffing.

Through the window alongside Mel's bed he could see Mynydd Troed. There was often snow at the top. He imagined being up there, plunging his hands into the snow, packing it tight in his fists. Looking down at the San, those parallel penitentiary rows on the hillside.

He would never be up there. He would never escape. He would die like Bobby. It would serve him right.

He'd been too scared to sit by Bobby's bed for fear of catching the bug.

The french windows stayed open to the snow. Fresh air was the thing. It was kill or cure. They all had red bedjackets, Sanatorium-issue. You wore them when you sat up to eat or do occupational therapy. Occupational therapy was making things like stuffed toys. Some were dab hands at it.

Others made model aircraft.

Some did a kind of tapestry.

Some did nothing.

Some went mad.

Bobby had gone mad, sort of. He'd had the bug first when he was very young, nine or ten, and they'd taken him away to somewhere called Highland Moors, but

24

he'd come home again and was never really cured. Then, when twenty-two, he had gone somewhere else and there a young man had died in the bed opposite, and it made Bobby ill in the head and they brought him home. He just followed Mam around all day, clinging to her, not letting her out of his sight. He hadn't been quite like other people before but now he was much worse. There was talk of him going to the mental hospital in Carmarthen.

Ralph used to sit at the back of the class, thinking of Bobby. The other kids didn't know what it was like; he felt separated from them by the misery of it all.

One night after supper Mam showed snapshots on the epidiascope, a sort of magic lantern, to take Bobby's mind off his private nightmare. It threw the pictures, much enlarged, on to the bedroom wall. One snapshot was of Mam and Dad, arm-in-arm in the garden. Bravely Mam sang:

> *Just like Darby and Joan*
> *In a world of their own*

just to try and cheer Bobby up. He got better in the head and worse in the body. And then came that bitter February day when he died.

One night the rain, driven by a high wind, came swamping into the ward. For once the french windows were banged shut; this was too close to nature, even for the San. Ralph stared at them, relishing the novelty of the sight.

Everything was cosier, everyone more relaxed. They were inside a womb and didn't want to come out. The rivulets of rain streaking down the window, the booming of the wind, belonged to an alien world. Mel joked with Ralph in a brotherly sort of way; Ralph wanted the storm to go on for ever.

At its height, Stan the domestic orderly—squat, round, red-faced—wheeled in their suppers on a trolley. Dishing up the salad, he slipped on the wet floor and the bowl went flying. Stan, shaken, scooped up the salad with his hands and put it back in the bowl.

'Anyone for beetroot?' he said.

2 Festivities

Christmas was coming. There was to be a concert in the Recreation Hall, put on by the boys on grades. Even those on bedrest could go, so long as they were allowed out of bed to go to the dubs. Ralph wasn't, because he was running a temperature. Only when this came down could he go to the dubs, and the concert.

Sister O'Neill peered at the thermometer.

'What is it, Sister?'

'Same as last night. 99 point four.'

99 point four was too high. 98 point 8 wasn't bad. 98 point six was better. 98 point four was perfect.

Going to the concert depended on a decimal.

A sudden change for the better: Jim moved out and Glyn moved in. Not that he had anything against Jim, except that he and Mel were big buddies.

Glyn was cool, friendly, clever; a medical student. The talk improved; fewer bints, tarts and tits.

Glyn spoke in a slow, considered way; already he was the embryonic consultant, telling outlandish medical tales with aplomb. He spoke of cadavers—never dead bodies—and of the penis of a dead man which had curved majestically, amazing all who saw it. A dignified note had been struck by the consultant who, awestruck, intoned, 'What a mag-ni-fi-cent penis!'

Glyn gave the words the weight and gravity they demanded. He was already master of the bedside manner.

O'Rorke lumbered into the ward every morning, carrying the world's news in a huge bag slung over his shoulder. He was big, monosyllabic, impenetrable, the only Irishman in Wales who never said six words when three would do.

Myopically he peered through his steel-rimmed glasses, pulling the papers from his bag like rabbits from a hat: *Mirror* for Mel, *Daily Mail* for John, *Manchester Guardian* for Glyn, *News Chronicle* for Ralph.

Wasn't he scared of catching the bug?

'I don't think he knows where he fucking is,' said Mel. 'He thinks he's somewhere healthy, like Pentonville.'

'He's become naturally immune through coming in here every day,' said Glyn judiciously.

'He's too bloody thick to catch anything,' said John.

Once a week, Glyn performed a strange ritual: he bought the *Picture Post* and plunged his nose into its glossy pages, coming up beatifically for air.

'I'd know it from its smell,' he said. 'Every paper is different.'

He was good at any kind of diagnosis.

Sundays began with cold ham; less smelly than haddock and more digestible than bacon.

Ralph knew he had to eat to get better. He weighed seven stone eight and you could count his ribs by just looking.

'You're painfully thin,' someone said, as if he didn't know it. Whose pain was it but his own?

They weren't all skinny in the San. Some were quite plump, and the boys on grades—who spent their time in the open air, hoeing and weeding and digging—looked much healthier than most of the people outside. But there were places of absolute quiet where the boys lay, cheeks fever-bright, their bodies giving out the sweet smell of corruption.

One night someone died on Block N. 'I knew it,' said Angus the orderly next morning. 'There was a dog howling all night. Did you hear it?'

He sounded almost pleased. It was part of life's drama.

Three days before Christmas, Ralph's temperature came down. Doctor John looked at his chart jovially.

'What do you think then, Sister? Shall we let him go to the concert?'

Sister O'Neill smiled noncommittally.

'If you keep your temp down you can go,' said Doctor John. 'But if it goes up again . . .'

'Thanks, doctor,' said Ralph.

Doctor John gave him a small, shy smile, put his hands behind his back and moved on.

'Now,' he said to Mel, 'how are you feeling in yourself?'

Everything was festive. There were paper chains, paper bells, sprigs of holly and mistletoe. Drink was still taboo but bottles were smuggled in and hidden away in bedside lockers, contraband from the foreign country that lay beyond the sanatorium gates.

Mel had a bottle of golden cream sherry.

'Fucking lovely,' he said. 'You ever tasted it?'

Ralph shook his head.

'Here you are,' said Mel. 'Try some.' He poured Ralph a generous tot in a glass.

'Go on,' he said. 'It'll do you good. Get it down you.'

Ralph had been brought up in the belief that strong drink was poison, even at Christmas. He put the glass to his lips and took a tentative sip. It glowed inside him, right down to his belly.

'You like it?' said Mel.

'Yeah. Great,' lied Ralph.

He sipped it again. Mel left him to it.

He remembered all he'd been told by his mother, about Iorrie next door dying of stomach cancer because of the beer he put away, about how bad they all were for you, beer and wine and spirits, *ach y fi*. He thought of his temperature going up again. He thought of the dog howling.

When Mel wasn't looking, he bent over his locker and poured the sherry into an empty cup.

'Enjoyed that, didn't you?' said Mel, smiling. 'Like another?'

'No thanks,' said Ralph. 'That was great. Fine. You drink it.'

Later, feeling ashamed, he took the cup to the dubs and flushed the sherry away.

Mam came to see him the weekend before Christmas. She brought him oranges and dates and presents to be opened on Christmas morning. She sat by his bed and talked of things back home. Home seemed a long time ago, although it was only three months.

'How's Dad?'

'He's fine. Sends his love. They all send their love, bach.'

Bobby had been dead for ten months now. He wondered how much of him was left, deep down in the grave.

On Christmas Eve, carol singers came up to the San from the village. They stood on the verandah outside the french windows, singing 'Hark the Herald Angels' and 'Silent Night' and 'O Come, All Ye Faithful.' They were boundlessly cheerful and said heartening things, though not coming too close.

It was a good clear night and the moon shone over the kitchen. He thought about his friends back at home, wondered what they were doing.

Some had sent cards. He arranged them on top of his locker.

One was from a girl who'd been in the same class as himself. He wondered why she'd sent it; they hadn't been friends, especially. It worried him, though he couldn't exactly say why.

He was glad when the carol singers went and the bell rang for lights out. He wanted some quiet, to think.

Christmas morning. He opened his presents: *Pickwick Papers* from his sister and a cricket book by Neville Cardus from his parents. There were sweets and chocolates and gift tokens and a board game from his brother in college.

He began reading *Pickwick Papers*. He'd hardly read any Dickens. His favourite author was Neville Cardus. His favourite cricketer was Denis Compton.

He handed the sweets round because such things were shared in the San.

They handed their sweets round to him.

They ate sweets and nuts all morning and then had their Christmas dinner. It was brought to them in bed, same as always, and they sat up to eat it from their trays.

They pulled Christmas crackers and wore funny hats.

They listened to the wireless and ate dates and walnuts.

They were all very friendly and pretended life was just normal.

After tea they put on their trousers and shirts and went to the concert.

It was strange being in a crowd. Everyone seemed to be talking at once. He was swamped by the noise. He was used to Ward 8 of Block M, with four voices only. Moreover he was afraid of getting worse through being out there. They should never have let him come; they should have known better.

He was sitting next to someone he didn't know; a boy about the same age as himself with cropped, sandy hair. He wondered which block he was on; how long he'd been in the San.

'Like one?' The boy offered him a wine gum from a packet.

'Thanks.' The one he took was dark; the colour of Ribena.

'Should be starting soon.'

'Hope so.'

'Been in here long?'

'Three months. And you?'

'I came in last week.'

'Last week! Just before Christmas.'

The boy said nothing. Ralph felt he'd said a stupid thing. He often said stupid things.

'Where you from then?' he asked, retrieving himself.

'Harlech. Where are you?'

'Aberystwyth.'

'Oh yes.'

'You been there?'

'Once. It rained all day.'

'Aye. it does sometimes.'

Another stupid thing.

'What block you on?'

'M,' the boy answered.

'That's funny. So am I.'

'I know. I've seen you.'

'Have you? I haven't seen you.'

'I know.' A smile, not unkind, flickered around the boy's mouth. 'I'm up the other end. Ward 2.'

The other end was another world; Ralph hardly ever went there.

'I've wandered down once or twice to your end,' the boy explained. 'I saw you with your headphones on.'

'Oh, did you?'

'Tell us your name then.'

'Ralph.'

'I'm Ken. Ken Black.'

Sudden applause and cheers; the entertainment began. It was good; some of it very good. The sketches were witty, well-acted. One even poked fun at Dr Kerrigan. Everyone roared. Ralph could just make out the back of her head in the front row. He imagined the small, tight smile on her face; the thin, rancid smile of a concentration camp guard.

No one poked fun at Jock; God is not mocked.

They walked back to Block M together, along the paved covered ways that threaded through the San. The songs and laughter filled Ralph's head; he was dazed with the noise and conviviality. It's like this outside all the time, he thought; down there, through those hospital gates. It was a weird notion, and then came another: I could just walk out, any time I like. There's nothing to stop me.

Nothing except the fear of death; nothing except the fear of ending up like Bobby.

3 Grey dust

The new year slunk in; they woke up to find things much the same as before. Mel stepped smartly to the dubs, whistling; John sat up in bed, hands clasped round his legs; Glyn sniffed the *Picture Post*; Ralph read a letter from home.

It came from his father, a self-taught artisan. He had possessed the brains to go to college but not the opportunity. He was part-time governors' clerk at the local grammar school, a job which meant beavering away at a big desk incongruously set in their tiny council house. There were times when no one could speak, when Dad was working. Once Dad went out after one of these strained, brittle hours, and everyone babbled with sheer relief, and Dad came suddenly back for something he'd forgotten.

He had looked at them reproachfully, as if they'd betrayed him.

Ralph felt the shame of it again, and put the letter back in its envelope.

'Hey, boys! There's German maids coming!'

The news fizzed round the San. It spelt romance, excitement. Who they were, why they came, nobody knew. It was enough that the girls were on their way, blonde frauleins with luscious lips who would give generously of themselves, spreading joy and light among the afflicted.

'Christ, I bet they've got tits out to by here! Bloody blind yourself on 'em, aye.'

'You tried putting a nipple in your ear? Bloody lovely it is.'

'I bet they go like rattlesnakes, mun, them Bavarians.'

'They do, boy. I been there, mun—in the fucking Army of Occupation, wasn't I?'

'Jesus fucking Christ, I'll be shagging the arse off 'em, aye!'

'Hey, Ralph. No tossing yourself off, right? We'll be watching your blankets tonight. If they move an inch we'll have 'em off and see what you're doing!'

He often had a hard-on at night. He left it alone. He had never masturbated in his life; he was innocent of many things, until he went to the San.

What worried him was not sex, or the absence of girl-friends, but worry itself. It was a demon burrowing into the back of his scalp, a hot crawling nastiness poisoning everything. He had known it first a few years ago, when he was ill in bed with something or other. He had been terrified, thinking he was going mad, unable to read or do anything to diminish the torment. Ever since, he had lived in dread of its return. And here it was again, an acute anxiety seeking a cause, ready to seize on anything to justify itself.

Rid of it, rid of it, he must get rid of it! He could tell no one; how could he? It would all sound so stupid. And they might send him to Carmarthen, lock him up, do anything.

Sister O'Neill stood over him sternly.

'Can't you manage more than that?' she said, seeing the tray he had pushed to the bottom of the bed.

'No sister, sorry.'

'You've got to eat to get better, you know.'

The worry took away his appetite, everything. It laid a grey dust over things which had hitherto pleased him. There was no joy, not one, which it did not corrupt and destroy. He knew that if it persisted, he would end up in Hospital Block.

The girl who'd sent a Christmas card began sending him magazines, with letters illicitly slipped between the pages. They were warm, friendly letters, not love letters at all. He'd always liked her, but now she seemed a threat. He felt she was trying to trap him, that if he got rid of her the worry would cease.

He felt this for many days until at last he wrote asking her never to write to him again, for fear that 'they might get too serious'.

In desperation he gave out the letter to be posted, knowing the stupidity of it.

The letter was posted and he turned over in bed, feeling ashamed.

He never heard from her again. But the worry went away.

His father sitting at the bedside, being cheerful. Ralph didn't know what to say.

'Who're you working for now then?' he managed at last.

'Oh, Mr Hughes—still the same.'

'Alright then, is it?'

'Well, it's a job.' Dad smiled. Ralph knew how much he hated the work.

'How's Mam?'

'Alright, bach. Fine. Hands aren't too good though, this time of year.'

'Oh—I'm sorry.'

Mam had arthritis; she didn't fuss, so he often forgot all about it.

'How about Joe? Still busy with the Wanderers?'

'Yes, they're doing well. Won 3-2 last Saturday.'

'Who against?'

'Y.M.'

'Still go there, do you?'

'Where, the football? No, I don't bother much.'

'I mean the Y.M.'

'Oh yes, I go there quite a lot. They've just made me Superintendent.'

He knew his father wanted him to ask about this, but he couldn't. The moment passed. Something else to feel guilty about.

There were some who came to the San and never left, even when they had beaten the bug. They took jobs around the place, lingering in this shadowy half-world because they could not face the hard light of the real world outside.

George the Greek was one of them. He ran the sub-post-office in the sanatorium grounds. He was short, brisk, loquacious, often coming around the wards of the bedridden to help or advise.

Walter was another. He had an elder-statesman look about him, tall, grizzled, dignified. He ran the sanatorium library and brought a selection of books around on a trolley. Walter was a Communist of the theological kind, believing not in bloody revolution but in gentle, priestly conversion.

Ralph found his presence reassuring. He knew he could always rely on him. And in an oblique way, he was a link with home: Walter had been a patient there the same time as Joe.

One day, Walter said, 'Have you read *The Good Companions*?'

'No, can't say I have.'

'I think you should—it's one of my favourite books. I'll bring it along if you like.'

'OK then.'

Ralph enjoyed it from the start, the man going off to the football match to cheer his heroes on. But he liked it most of all because it was about someone who breaks free. It was something he longed to do himself—break free and start living. He had been in the San long enough. He wanted to go home.

'We're going to give you an AP,' said Doctor John.

He stood at the end of the bed, passing the verdict, smiling faintly, looking apologetic. Sister O'Neill clutched the files, tits appetisingly bulging.

'Which side?' asked Ralph.

'The right,' said the doctor. 'We'll do it next Tuesday, OK?'

'OK.' He didn't have much choice but was more pleased than sorry. At least they were trying something;

and in the strange hierearchy of the San, it would give him some kind of status.

Mel gloated; Glyn consoled; John took little notice. And next day, John was taken to Hospital Block.

AP stood for artificial pneumothorax, a way of collapsing the lung by pumping air into the chest through a hypodermic needle. It was not half so drastic as a thora, which entailed major surgery and was viewed as the last desperate throw of the dice. You went somewhere else for one of those, and if you survived you had a hero's welcome on your return—a VC in the war against the bug.

'Bet they give John a thora,' said Mel.

'They might and they might not,' said Glyn, in his measured way.

'Bet they fucking do.' Mel looked at Ralph. 'They may give you a fucker too, if the AP doesn't work.'

He tried to take no notice of Mel now. And he wasn't afraid of the needle.

John's empty bed made them uncomfortable, as if someone had died. They averted their eyes; even Glyn was affected. He was fractious with Mel and, still missing Jim, Mel was vituperative in return. Mel said he would ask to go somewhere fucking else. It was a novel idea; such transfers were rare. Not defined enough even to be an unwritten rule, there was a general sense that to move wards was a copping out, a failure to stand up to the test. It was not nearly as bad, though, as leaving the San without being properly discharged. A poor view was taken of this; those who did so were expected to come to a bad end, and tales were told with a morbid relish of deserters dying within months, having in their folly spurned the corporate wisdom and *esprit de corps* of the San.

'Right. Now lie on your left side, and put your right hand behind your head.'

Doctor John smiled encouragingly, cheeks farmer-pink. Sister O'Neill looked at Ralph; she too was smiling.

Ralph turned on his side, right arm raised behind his head, out of the way of the needle. 'Good. Now just a little pin-prick. Keep breathing steadily.'

The needle went into his side, just below the armpit; it had been shaved clean the night before. 'Good. Keep steady now.' He lay quite still, thinking of the stories he had heard of things going wrong, both lungs totally collapsing. He felt the needle in his side, a certain pressure, but that was all; no real discomfort. Attached to the needle was a length of rubber tubing connecting with two bottles fastened to a wooden framework. The way the bottles were moved up and down mysteriously provided the pressure that pumped air through the tubing into the chest.

Doctor John jiggled the bottles, calling out figures from time to time which Sister O'Neill jotted down. These, Ralph knew, were something to do with air pressures. He lay still, very still; all must be going well. At last Doctor John said, 'Good man,' and took out the needle. He rubbed the spot where it had been with cotton wool; something stung a little.

'That's it then. Feel alright?' He smiled down at Ralph.

'Yes, fine.'

'You can put your arm down now. Just lie there a minute.'

He turned on to his back and looked up at the ceiling. Sister O'Neill clattered the Emmet-like contraption into a corner. Doctor John made some notes in his file.

'We'll give you a refill the day after tomorrow and then it will be one a week.'

'It's OK then, is it?'

'Yes. Everything's fine. We'll give you a screening in a couple of weeks to make sure it's taken alright.'

Another smile, straight from the fatstock auction.

'We'll take you back to your ward now. Well done.'

They took him back in a wheelchair; had to be careful at first.

John's bed was empty for five days, and then it was taken over by Iorrie. He was nineteen years old, sandy-haired, cheerful. He came from Blaenau Ffestiniog and had worked in a quarry, which he pronounced to rhyme with 'Larry.'

Iorrie sang a lot, the popular songs of the day. He would stand by the door of the ward, in his slippers and dressing-gown, looking up and down the corridor. There did not appear to be a great deal wrong with him; he was clearly a dandruff case.

Then came the German maids. The most charismatic was Trudy, who had blonde hair, big breasts and a suspiciously high colour. 'Bet she's got the bug herself,' said the barrack-room doctors wisely.

Trudy scurried up and down Block M, irridescently

cheerful. Her smiles, her buoyancy, her ardent eagerness to please, were a kind of war reparation. Soon it became known that Don Hull was taking a particular interest in her. He was even more of a dandruff case than Iorrie; it was hard to believe there was anything wrong with him that a brisk walk would not cure.

'He had her in bed with him last night. Angus was telling me.'

'Don't be daft. He couldn't have, not on this block.'

'He did, I tell you. Angus said.'

'If you believe Angus, you'll believe any bugger.'

Angus was a bullish nursing orderly with a shiny bald head and brawny arms, still powerful in his middle to late fifties. His features were coarse, his most frequent expression one of sullen resentment. When he made a bed he tucked in the blankets fiercely, as if to straitjacket its occupant. Occasionally he perked up to sing, very softly, barrack-room ballads of impressive obscenity. These cheered him considerably; the more degenerate the song, the brighter his spirits.

Angus often worked in tandem with Dai, who was better tempered and less intensely crude. They made beds at breakneck speed, Angus on one side and Dai on the other. Then there was Ken, a tall, indolent man who did the patients small favours, as if he actually appeared to like them. Later came Derek, who was perfumed and distinctly odd. It took some time for Ralph to understand the precise nature of his oddity.

The nursing orderlies were a rung above the domestics, who cleaned the wards and served the food. Hilda was one of these. She shuffled around looking defeated and

43

exchanging tired vulgarities with the patients. Although genial in a worn-out sort of way she had one overpowering disadvantage: she ponged. Hilda gave lack of hygiene a bad name.

Yet there was still life of a kind in her. Once, grotesquely kittenish, she brandished the handle of her sweeping brush in front of Ralph, as if to belabour him with it.

'Piss off!' exploded Ralph.

'What?' cried Hilda, astonished. 'You can't say that to me. I could report you for that, I could.'

She made some token sweeps of the brush and slip-slopped out of the ward, cloaked in tattered dignity.

'Fancy saying that,' said Mel unctuously. 'I've never told any woman to piss off.'

'Depends who the woman is,' said Glyn drily.

Ralph slunk down beneath the sheets, feeling ashamed; after six months in the San he had no clear grasp any more of what was acceptable and what wasn't.

Mel, Glyn, Iorrie, Ralph.

He felt it might go on for ever: Mel being spiteful, Glyn sniffing *Picture Post*, Iorrie singing silly, innocent songs, himself feeling miserable.

He could not believe he would ever get better.

The weather grew colder. The radiators banged away in the middle of the night. 'Airlocks,' people said carelessly, as if they were as much an act of God as the frost and the wind and the bug. Nothing was done.

There was nothing to do about anything.

Mynydd Troed was now one sheet of white. Like Bobby's shroud. He thought of him lying there, abandoned.

When the grave was filled in a large stone had been left lying on top. It was immediately over the place where Bobby's head must be, as he lay there in his coffin. He had imagined the stone pressing down on his forehead and Bobby suffering even yet.

He had wanted to take the stone away but dared not.

A letter from Mam. She wrote every week, giving him all the news in a homely, innocent way. He felt a million years away from all she was talking about.

Mel, Glyn, Iorrie, Ralph.

Ralph, Glyn, Iorrie, Mel.

The news of John was not good. He was on Absolute and Blocks.

Ralph pictured him lying there, his head much lower than his feet, the bed tilted up by those dreaded blocks of wood placed under its legs. No one quite knew why because no one was told very much.

But everyone knew that blocks were bad news.

They were only one step away from a thora.

4 News from Nowhere

The AP took. His temperature stayed down so he was
able to walk to an adjacent block for refills every week.
He lay on his left side, with his right hand behind his
head, and Dr John stuck in the needle and jiggled the
bottles and Sister O'Neill wrote figures in the file he
was never allowed to see.

On his way back to Ward 8 he sometimes looked in
on Ken Black. It was strange down that end of Block M,
almost like a foreign country. Ralph would have loved to
be there, in the same ward as this unexpected new
friend. But he could not ask for a move; as well ask for
Mynydd Troed to turn green and sprout olives.

And then a sudden change: Mel was taken off bedrest
and put on hours. He was allowed to get dressed and
walk around for an hour or two a day, and play cards in
the dayroom, and stroll down to the shop to buy stuff
from George the Greek.

The boys on hours looked strange. They had crossed a
frontier, moving out of the democracy of pyjamas into
a new social order. Having clothes on made them
aristocrats. They incited envy and jealousy.

This was the one great step towards freedom. For
when you were allowed up all day, you moved out of
Block M to a different part of the San. You were on your
way. Bedrest was for the lower orders.

Ralph was glad to see Mel put on hours because it
meant that soon, he would be rid of him entirely.

46

Winter grew still more wintry. The boys pulled their red bedjackets tightly around themselves when they sat up in bed.

They blew air from their diseased lungs and saw it crystallise into clouds.

They were allowed to wear mittens to ward off chilblains or, perhaps, frostbite. They were not allowed to wear vests under their pyjama tops. But some did, secretly.

Ralph was making stuffed toys. It was a way of passing the time and approved as occupational therapy. He was not very good at it.

He tried making replicas of Bambi, Disney's poignant young deer. They sagged pitifully, or bulged in odd places, and his stitching was so poor that the stuffing usually poked through like grey, fluffy entrails.

Mel had been very good at making 'cameo' brooches in a neat, workmanlike way. But, like childish things, these had been put behind him now he was on hours.

Glyn did nothing like this. He read a great deal, or listened to the Home Service on the headphones. He had the air, not so much of being ill, as of biding his time.

Iorrie wandered up and down the corridors all day in his dressing-gown, far more often than the call of nature demanded. He was rarely in his own bed but usually squatting on somebody else's, animatedly chatting, scurrying back to Ward 8 at the approach of a doctor or sister.

He appeared to have boundless energy and to be there under false pretences.

He cheered Ralph up no end.

In the Great World Beyond, Attlee's Labour Government grappled with shortages and rationing and the Communist Threat and the constant sniping of Churchill and the Tory Press. Nearly all the boys were Labour, many of them coming from the coal communities of South Wales where even a donkey could get to Parliament by joining the Party, so people said.

John had been a true-blue, believing that everyone could Get On if they tried.

'Everyone can't be ambitious,' Mel argued.

'Of course they can,' John insisted.

Ralph wondered who John was arguing with now. What opportunity *was* there for argument? He was in a single-bed cell in Hospital Block, coughing quietly into his hankie, gobbing discreetly into his sputum pot.

John would never give any trouble if he could help it.

News from Nowhere; Syd Berry was dead. Rumour had it that he had been a rebel, defying the Great White Chief Jock to his very face. Consequently he had been expelled from the San, to meet the inevitable fate.

It was told as a morality tale.

Ralph thought of Bobby.

There were more rumours about Don Hull and Trudy. Don did not deny them; why should he? They made him a person of consequence. He swaggered down the corridor to the dubs, looking devil-may-care and fulfilled. He was a playboy in pyjamas.

His charm appeared to work on Sister O'Neill. She

turned a blind eye to things she would have censured in others.

But Block M woke up one morning to find Trudy no longer there. And something was missing from Don Hull's swagger.

In the third week of February, benign winds blew from the south. Mynydd Troed was green again. O'Rorke whistled as he hulked around, delivering the papers. Spring seemed but a breath away.

There was a jauntiness about Doctor John as he went his rounds; perhaps the lambing was going well. He was more inclined to lift patients up a rung than put them down; the number of those on hours increased. Importantly they put on their clothes and went to the day room. For those left behind, the empty beds were a reprimand. Ralph half expected to receive a report saying, 'Could do better. Must try harder.'

The news from home was good. Aber were top of the league and progressing well in the Amateur Cup. Eddie Ellis looked like setting up a goalscoring record and Howard Williams was brilliant between the posts. Teddy Bevan had scored with a free kick from the half-way line. The club had a new centre-half from South Wales.

All this from Billy, who kept up his loyal if less frequent correspondence. There was other news as well.

Piggy Charles has gone to teach in Birmingham, thank goodness. Lets hope he stays there and good riddance. I had detention from Titch Roberts for talking in class. Glenys Thomas and Ray Jones went in the girls toilets together one day last week. They were nearly caught by Lally Powell coming out. I'll be leaving in the summer to start my apprenticeship. You'll be home by then I expect. Sorry I can't come to see you but its too far. Anyway thats all for now so I'll close.

Your old pal,
Billy.

Billy was the only one who wrote to him, apart from his family. The girl he had told not to write wouldn't again, ever.

He wondered how he'd face her when he got out. If he ever did.

'How are you this long time then?'

Ken Black, cheerfully sticking his head round the door.

'Hiya! Come in.'

'I suppose I have to come and see you if you don't see me.'

'I did, the other day.'

'Only for a minute.'

Ken came in and sat on his bed.

'What's that ugly thing you're making?'

'A bambi.'

'Looks more like a dying duck. All the inside's coming out.'

'I know, I can't get it to stay in somehow.'

'Better give up and try something else.'

'Do you do these things?'

'Not likely. I don't do anything. Except read.' He picked up *The Good Companions*. 'What's this like?'

'Not bad. Very good, in fact.'

'What's it about?'

'Oh . . . a man who leaves home to join some people . . . actors and that.'

Ken read a sentence or two at random. 'I might try it myself. Let me have it when you've finished, will you?'

'OK.'

They chatted awhile. Ken spoke quietly, without a noticeable accent. His father had moved to Harlech from somewhere in England; Ralph gathered he was a professional man of some kind. He never mentioned his mother. His light blue eyes were alert, his manner an odd mixture of diffidence and curiosity. He was not painfully thin like Ralph; you could not have told, from looking at him, that he was ill at all.

Mel made steady progress.

'I'll be off this cunting block soon,' he announced one day. 'They're moving me down to Block F.'

He looked across at Ralph.

'I'll leave you to your wanking pit, you fucking Aberystwyth asshole,' he said amiably.

On his very last day in the ward, a ceremony took place. Mel took a small, tattered Union Jack from behind his bed and handed it over to Ralph.

The flag was traditionally held by the patient who had been in the ward the longest.

'See you don't keep the fucker too long,' said Mel,

with a look that had in it the merest hint of big-brotherly concern.

'I won't, don't worry,' said Ralph unconvincingly.

'Wonder who we'll have next,' said Glyn. He sniffed the *Picture Post* speculatively.

It was Ronnie who came. He was short, with slicked-down black hair and glasses. He was from Rhyl, and had served in the Pioneer Corps in the war. His smooth, oriental-looking face was unmarked by experience. He came into the ward, looking neither to left nor right, got into bed and put on his headphones.

That is how he remained. Interruptions for eating or going to the dubs were minimal. He was the most steadfastly horizontal patient in the San, outside those on Absolute. Antennaed with headphones, he lay there placidly for hour upon hour, staring up at the ceiling as he listened to the Light Programme's trite succession of dance bands and comedians.

'What do you think about all day?' inquired Glyn, stung out of his normal demeanour of philosophical acceptance.

'I don't think about anything.'

'You can't think of nothing. It isn't possible.'

'Yes it is,' argued Ronnie virtuously.

'You must be a moron.'

Ronnie slid down again between the sheets, contentedly clamping on his headphones.

'He doesn't even bloody know what a moron is,' said Glyn despairingly.

Ralph's condition stabilised. He felt he wasn't getting any worse, yet he wasn't any better either. His weight remained seven stone eight. Sister O'Neill, her full breasts tantalisingly close, wrote the figures down as he stepped off the scales.

He hardly ever thought about what he might do for a living some day. All ambition was contained within the compass of the San. In class-system terms the bedrest patients were the proles, the lowest of the low; the boys on the final, sixth grade were the aristocrats, doing harder physical work than most people outside. Between lay the careful gradations that marked one's ascent up the ladder, and all the uncertainty of progress of the social climber: here, too, one was forever on the brink of a chasm, liable to plunge back into the depths if one's foothold failed.

The biggest step was the first, the promotion from bedrest to hours. It was a dream, an impossible dream for some, who languished in a twilight world as the bug burrowed deeper, poisoning their skeletal bodies. For others, very ill but with hope, it was a distant dream. They attained it after two years, three years, four years; old campaigners in the war, they earned the respect of their comrades, and when discharged at last they had a hero's send-off.

To get out, to get out! To get up every day, walk around, go on buses and trains, do as one wished! This was the one purpose in life. When he did project himself into the vagueness beyond, Ralph thought perhaps of being a journalist . . . or an accountant. He was good with words, good with figures. The one thing he knew was that he would never go back to school.

April 30, 1949. He had been there exactly six months. They had promised him he would be home in six months.

He would never again believe anything anyone told him.

Home . . . Mam doing the washing, wringing the blankets out with sturdy brown arms, the old mangle in the backyard rusting away with neglect. Mam, so strong yet so gentle.

And growing older. She would be sixty-two in November. He was the child of her middle age.

The thought of her dying belonged to the world of nightmare.

Dad, going to work early. Singing in the church choir. Organising classes in the YM.

Joe, going to work in an office.

Number 18, Riverside Row. Redbrick council houses looking out over the river that ebbed and flowed with the tide. Always the seagulls soaring and gliding, swooping to catch crusts of bread in mid-flight, pecking the potato peelings slung over the wall where people sat for a neighbourly chat.

Mrs Evans, Mrs Jones, Mrs Jenkins, Mrs Prendergast. He saw them all, in the piercing light of his longing.

He was not so much homesick as lonely inside. He had changed so much already, he could never get back to what he had been.

5 Mickey Mouse

When Iorrie moved out, the worst thing of all happened. Des Collins took his place. He swaggered into the ward, with the boundless self-confidence of the braggart. After putting on pyjamas he sat up straight in bed, arms linked round his knees, boldly taking command. His face might have been handsome had it not been so coarse. His light blue eyes, flecked with a blend of arrogance and suspicion, coldly took in his new surroundings. Ralph soon knew he had an enemy.

'What's that book you're reading?' he asked tauntingly.

'Neville Cardus.'

'What's it about?'

'Cricket.'

'*Cricket*! You don't like cricket, do you?'

'Yes. Why, don't you?'

'You being funny, *Ralphie*?'

It was always 'Ralphie,' uttered with contempt. Des set out to humiliate him. He mocked everything Ralph said or did, seized on every chance to disparage his home and family.

'Don't come to see you very often, do they?' he sneered, when his own visitors had left one weekend.

'They can't. It's too far away.'

'They can come and stay round here, can't they?'

'They can't afford it very often.'

'Can't afford it? What's your father do then?'

'He's a painter and decorator.'

'Painter and decorator!' jeered Des. 'What a failure.'

'No he's not!'

'Don't you tell *me* what he is, Ralphie. If I say he's a failure he's a fucking failure, right?'

Des's conceit was so profound as to be sublime. He held, for himself, a Hollywood glamour and his burnished ego was impervious to the rough humour of the San.

'Tell me, boys,' he said, lovingly combing his wavy blond hair one afternoon. 'What film star do I remind you of?'

The silence was broken by Glyn.

'Mickey Mouse,' he said.

Ralph knew he should stand up more to Des, but could not. He neither humiliated himself by trying to placate him, nor struck out in protest. He simply absorbed the hurt, miserable and ashamed. He became more ill, such energy as he possessed being expended on this inner loathing of Des. He hated his taunting blue eyes, shit-yellow hair, brown patterned dressing-gown, glutinous voice. Des was a crooner manqué, a Dick-Haymes-to-be denied fame only by a temporary quirk of fate.

> *Sentimental me*
> *Guess I'll always be . . .*

The sugary sentimentality of these ballads contrasted strangely with the crudity of the grubby, badly-printed 'books' he passed around the ward.

'Go on Ralphie, read this. It's hot stuff. Full of shagging. But if I catch you wanking, I'll kill you, you cunt.'

Ralph glanced at a few pages, then put it aside.

56

'Don't like it. Sorry.'

'Don't like it? Don't fucking like it? Who are you to say if you fucking like it or not.'

Des swung his legs out of bed and pulled back Ralph's bedclothes.

'Look, he's wanking! He's fucking wanking, the tosser!'

'No I'm not.'

'Yes, you fucking are.'

Ralph pulled the bedclothes back up in outrage because he wasn't doing anything, didn't even have a hard-on.

'I hate you,' he cried passionately.

'Do you then? Oh there's a shame. Hear what he said, boys? The poor little shithouse hates me.'

'Leave him alone,' said Glyn mildly. 'He's not doing any harm.'

'Useless little cunt,' spat Des venomously, snatching the book back.

Every so often Dr John saw the boys on Block M individually, in a small room by the entrance where Ralph had said goodbye to his mother, a lifetime ago. It was a time for reviewing progress, or the lack of it; for imparting nuggets of information in a tight, controlled way.

'How am I getting along?' asked Ralph.

'Quite well, quite well,' said Doctor John with the bright, febrile smile he gave animals bound for the abattoir. 'But your weight could be a bit better, couldn't it?'

'I can't help that,' said Ralph defensively, feeling he was being blamed.

'It's very important to eat all the food you're given. You do that, don't you?'

'As much as I can.'

'You should try and eat it all,' said Doctor John automatically.

Pink, preoccupied, he tapped his fingers on the table. Ralph's chart was before him. He turned a page and coughed.

'We think we might have to try something more. Just to help you along.'

'What are you going to try?' asked Ralph. 'Not a thora?'

'Oh no, not—' Ralph knew the word he cut off, last-second, was 'yet.'

'We aren't thinking about a thora,' said Doctor John carefully.

'What then?'

'Perhaps a PP. We'll give it a month or two.' Another water-colour smile, easily washed away.

'I *am* making progress though, am I?'

'Oh yes, you're coming along well. It's just that—'

'You're not thinking of moving me?'

'Moving you?'

'To Hospital Block.'

'Good heavens no. What makes you think that?'

'Just wondering. How is John getting along there?'

'John?'

'Bowen. He used to be with us.'

'Oh, John Bowen. Fine. He's coming along fine.'

'I want a move myself,' said Ralph desperately.

'*You* want a move?'

'Yes.'

'Whatever for?'

'I'm not happy where I am. There's someone in Ward 8 I hate.'

Another smile, this time of amusement. 'Hate? That's a strong word, Ralph.'

'I want to move this end of the block. I don't want to stay where I am.'

'Can't do that, I'm afraid. Everywhere's full. There aren't any empty beds just now.'

'But when there is,' persisted Ralph. 'Can I move then?'

'If you like. We'll see how you feel then, shall we? You might have changed your mind by then.'

Ralph gave up. He knew it was always going to be like this.

Midsummer madness. Dai Evans claimed to have shagged Nurse Graham in the storeroom. 'Her arse was bumping the door. Didn't you hear it?' He was triumphant, his tubercular flush deeper.

Bert Lane, lanky ex-corporal, was stuffing a girl from the village behind the Handicrafts Shed at night. Someone had seen them at it. 'Christ, he was going like a train. No wonder the bugger's knackered.'

On stifling days the boys sweated and took off pyjama jackets. 'Put them back on, please,' ordered Sister O'Neill primly. 'That's not allowed.'

'Why, Sister? It's roasting in here, mun!'

'It's bad for you to be bare-chested.'

'But we aren't out in the sun!' Sunshine on bare chests was known to be bad for those with the bug.

'Never mind. Do as you're told.'

They put them back on resignedly, then took them off again when she'd gone.

In the still, heat-clotted ward Des talked dirty. He disgorged tales of his sexual adventures. 'I was sucking her tits and she was moaning like fuck and then I got my fingers up her quim and . . .'

Ronnie, catching some of this in one of the brief moments when his headphones were off, took an interest and did not put them on again.

'I had a smashing girl one night in Llandudno,' he said, cow-brown eyes round and solemn. 'I took her up the Orme, we had a hell of a good time.'

'Sure it was Llandudno?' said Glyn. 'Not Bombay?'

'No, this was Llandudno. I've been to Bombay as well.'

'Wonder you know the difference.'

'You being funny or something?'

'What makes you think that, Ronnie?'

'Sounds like you are.'

'Not me. Life's too short.' Glyn put the opened-out *Picture Post* to his nose and inhaled deeply, luxuriously.

Des turned his brute head to Ralph. 'Don't suppose you've ever seen a naked woman, Ralphie. Wouldn't know what it was. You'd think her prick had been cut off, wouldn't you?'

'Oh, shut up. Leave me alone.'

'Leave me alone,' mimicked Des. 'Leave me alone or I'll run home to Mammy.'

Mam pegging clothes on the line, bending down to take another sopping shirt from the wicker-basket on the garden path. Ill at home, waiting for a vacant bed in the San, he had heard her singing outside, sometimes the songs he had composed in his head.

> *It's too late*
> *To say I love you,*
> *Too late*
> *To change my mind . . .*

She was the most cheerful of skivvies, crawling with duster in hand to whisk away the under-bed fluff, bringing his meals up on a tray, sitting sewing as he read out the news of the day, taking away the sick-smelling sheets he fouled by spouting his food out.

'When's she coming to see you next, Ralphie?' taunted Des.

'Who?'

'Who d'you think? Your mother, of course.'

'Next month, I think.'

'You think! If she remembers, that is.'

'What's that?'

'Oh, nothing.' Des turned his back, knowing he'd gone too far.

Ralph knew he should jump on him, hit him, kill him for the insult to his mother.

He turned the other way and closed his eyes. Glyn sniffed the *Picture Post*. Ronnie lay back, listening to the wireless.

Glyn was next to be promoted to hours. He dressed punctiliously and walked with a neat, professional air between the ward and the dayroom, looking far more the practised medico than Doctor John. Ralph tried to be glad for his sake but it meant that he was more exposed than ever to Des's bullying.

Curiously, Des left Ronnie alone. Ronnie lay forever locked in his dreamy paradise, headphones clamped on, listening to Joe Loss and Geraldo and Billy 'Mr Wakey-Wakey' Cotton. He often smiled a faint baby smile, as if he needed to have his back patted to bring the wind up. Even in his most miserable moments Ralph did not envy Ronnie his happiness, because he knew it was based on the most implacable stupidity.

Ralph had been fond of swing bands for years, but now he much preferred jazz. He listened to Jazz Club on the wireless every Saturday evening; so, it turned out, did Ken Black. Ralph liked trad, Ken modern jazz. They had fierce arguments that raised Ralph's spirits but which Des listened to with rancorous envy.

'Proper know-all, that mate of yours,' he said, after Ken had gone back to his ward. 'He knows fuck-all about anything really.'

'He knows a lot about jazz,' said Ralph stoutly.

'Jazz? Who wants to know anything about jazz? It's a load of balls.'

'No it's not.'

'Yes it is. Tommy Dorsey and Gene Krupa, *that's* proper music. Not your fucking Louis Armstrong and Jelly Roll Morton and all that shit.'

'It's very clever music,' said Ralph. 'It's all improvised —they play as the mood takes them.'

'Sounds like it,' said Des. 'By Christ. Jungle music, that's all it is. Played by a lot of black bastards.'

'There's nothing wrong with being black.'

'Oh, one of them, are you? Trust you, Ralphie. Fucking wanker. I've seen your bedclothes shake at night.'

'No they don't.'

'Yes they do. That's why you're so skinny. Wanking yourself to death.'

It wasn't true. But no use telling Des.

One Saturday afternoon he had an unexpected visitor. She stood hesitantly at the half-open door into the ward. Black hair, brown eyes, slim. About his age. A total stranger.

'You Ralph Lloyd?'

'Yes.'

'I'm Morwen Phillips. Cherry Farm. Your mother stays with us when she's down here.'

'Oh. Hullo.'

He stared at her.

'Ask her in, Ralph, for God's sake,' said Glyn kindly.

'Oh. Yes. Come on in.'

She stood awkwardly by his bed. 'My mother told me to bring you this. Some home-made cakes.'

'Oh. That's nice. Thanks.' He took the packet from her.

They looked at each other, lost in mutual shyness.

'You feeling better?' she asked.

'Yes thanks. I'm coming along.'

'That's good.'

'Takes a long time though.'

'I know. How long you been in here for now?'

'Nine months, nearly.'

'I'm sorry.'

Her prettiness startled him.

'Sit down for a minute, won't you?' he said.

'OK then. I can't stay long though.' She walked round the bed to the wooden chair the other side, next to his locker. She gave him a brief glance, smiling, then looked down, a faint blush staining her lightly-tanned cheeks.

'How's your mother then?' he asked.

'Fine. And yours?'

'OK. She's coming down next month, to see me.'

'I know. She's staying with us. You used to yourself when your brother was in here, didn't you?'

'Aye, that's right. You remember then!' he said, surprised.

'Course I do. You used to help me feed my pet rabbit.'

Ralph laughed. 'That's right. What's his name now?'

'Monty. He's dead now.'

'Oh, is he? I'm sorry.'

'That's alright. He was a bit old really.'

'Was he?'

'Got quite bad in the end. His fur fell out and he wouldn't eat.'

'There's a shame.' The not-eating made him feel an affinity with Monty. 'Got another I suppose now, have you?'

'Another what?' She looked startled.

'Rabbit.'

64

'No. Never. Not after Monty.'

'Oh, no. Course not,' he said, feeling stupid. 'You wouldn't want to, I don't suppose.'

'You got any pets? At home?'

'No, nothing. Just as well. I wouldn't be able to look after them now, would I?'

'No, but your family could, couldn't they?'

'Yes, I suppose.'

'Your brother would, I'm sure.'

Yes, Joe would. He would do anything.

'I remember him. He's nice. Does he come to see you much?'

'No, not much. He can't really. He's too busy.'

Thinking of Joe made him feel homesick. She looked at his downcast eyes and felt awkward again.

'Well, I'll be going then,' she said soon after.

'Oh, can't you stay a bit longer?'

'No, I can't now.' She stood up. 'I'll come again. If you like.'

'Yes. I would.'

He looked up at her, not knowing what to do. Shake her hand? Her brown eyes held something he did not understand.

'Right then. See you,' she said.

'Who the fuck was that bint you had with you?' asked Des later, after his visitors had gone.

'She wasn't a bint.'

'What was she then, Ralphie? A fucking bloke in disguise?'

'She was a girl, that's what.'

'Get away! I wouldn't have known.'

Ralph, his insides tight, stared at Des, challenging.

'Didn't know what to fucking do with her,' said Des, backing off. 'That's your trouble.'

He slid down in the bed, turning his back.

Glyn looked at Ralph and winked.

Ralph knew he had scored a small but important victory.

6 Weight Watching

In August Mel came around, saying goodbye. He was going home.

It was the tradition for boys being released to go around the blocks where they had done their bedrest, shaking hands with everyone, whether they knew them or not. They wore their best clothes, for going home was the biggest event anyone could imagine.

Mel looked strange in his dark suit, like a bridegroom in search of a wedding.

He shook hands with Glyn, then Ronnie, then Des. He stood by Ralph's bed.

'Well,' he said. 'Still here then?'

'Looks like it,' said Ralph cheerfully.

'How long's it been now?'

'Ten months nearly.'

'Only one of us lot left then.'

'That's right.'

'Time you got on hours then, isn't it?'

Ralph said nothing.

'Fucking Aberystwyth asshole,' Mel said kindly.

Dear Ralph, wrote Billy,

I hope your feeling better now. I've been working for over a month and like it though the boss is a bit grumpy. Never mind its better than school.

I've signed for Penparcau in the Junior League and hope to get a few games at outside-left, though I can play left-half as well. Betty Pratt's been asking after you again. We thought you'd be home by now. Sorry I can't come and see you but its too far.

Your old pal,
Billy.

There was no more talk from Doctor John of more radical treatment. Ralph dared not ask in case it reminded him. He trudged over for refills every week, listened to the wireless, read his books.

August gave way to September. He was 17 on the 8th.

'I'm going home,' said Ronnie suddenly, sitting up in bed.

'You can't,' said Glyn gravely. 'You're not even on hours yet.'

'Yes I can. There's nothing to stop me.'

Glyn stood by his wardrobe, carefully putting on his tie.

'I can leave any time I like,' said Ronnie. He sounded agitated, the contrast with his normally comatose state startling.

'It wouldn't be very wise,' said Glyn. 'You wouldn't get proper treatment at home.'

'Treatment? You call this treatment? They're not doing anything.'

'You're resting. If you needed anything else they'd give it you.'

'I'm sick of this place. I'm sick of you. I'm sick of everyone.' He looked around the ward wildly. 'I can't stay here another minute, you understand? I've got to get out.'

He threw back the blankets and opened his wardrobe door. He began throwing clothes on his bed.

'Don't be stupid,' said Glyn, grasping his wrist.

'Lay off me, you!'

'You can't leave. Don't be stupid.'

'Yes I fucking can. Yes I fucking *can*.'

'You're mad.'

'Turn your fucking back. I'm going to get dressed.'

'I'll call for Sister,' threatened Glyn. There was a bell beside each bed.

'It won't make any difference. She can't stop me.' Ronnie tore off his pyjama jacket and put on a pale yellow vest with short sleeves.

Glyn rang the bell.

'What the fuck's happening?' Llew from Ward 9, black-haired, whimsical, poked his head round the door.

'This silly bugger says he's leaving,' said Glyn.

'Where's he going?'

'Home, so he says.'

'Fuck me.'

Llew went over to Ronnie. He was buttoning his shirt up.

'What's up, Ronnie?'

'Nothing. I'm just going home, that's all.'

'Where d'you live?'

'Rhyl.'

'Long way. How you gonna get there?'

'Train, of course. What d'you think?'

'They expecting you then? Told them, have you?'

'No, course I fucking haven't. I've only just decided, haven't I?'

'Be a bit of a shock for them, won't it? They won't have your bed ready.'

'Don't be daft! They won't mind.'

'Won't they?'

'No, they fucking—'

'They'll be worried sick when they see you. You're supposed to be here. They won't know what to do.'

Ronnie looked dazed, fumbled with his cuffs.

'They'll be scared, Ronnie. Real scared.'

'What d'you mean, scared?'

'Scared for you. They'll think you've signed your death warrant.'

'Don't talk wet!'

'I mean it, Ronnie. Look. Why are you here?'

'I don't fucking know!'

'Yes you do. You've got the fucking bug, haven't you? That's why they sent you here. To get better.'

Ronnie looked helplessly down at the heap of clothes on his bed.

'You've got to stick it, mun. You've got to beat the bastard.'

'I can do that at home!'

'No you can't. You know what will happen? You'll be going out with your mates. You'll be getting pissed. You'll start mopping. You'll frighten your mother to fuck. And you'll give her the bug. And your dad. And your fucking brothers and sisters, if you've got any. You'll give them all the bug because you're too fucking selfish to stay here.'

'Don't you call me that!' cried Ronnie, close to tears.

'Well, act your age for fuck's sake and get back in bed.'

'Fucking hell.' Ronnie sat heavily on the edge of the bed. He buried his face in his hands.

Sister O'Neill stepped primly through the french windows.

'What's up?' she said.

Llew put his finger to his lips. Sister O'Neill stared at Ronnie, then Llew. Silently she withdrew.

'You'll be alright, pal,' Llew said gently. 'You're only a fucking dandruff case. You'll be out of here in six months. But you can't jump the gun. Understand?'

Ronnie nodded.

'We're all in the same fucking boat. But you can't get out on your own or you're lost.' He put his arm round Ronnie's shoulders. 'Back to bed then, yes? I'll come in later—play you crib, OK?'

Llew went back to his ward. Ronnie undressed and put on his pyjamas.

He got back in bed and lay on his side, not even listening to the wireless.

Then, the impossible. Des was sentenced to Hospital Block.

They took him away in a wheelchair because an X-ray had shown up something bad. He went with a brave smile, the archetypal B-movie hero.

'Wish me luck, Ralphie boy. Come and see me, won't you?'

'If I can.'

'Bet you'll forget all about me, you cunt.'

He stretched out a hand. It was limp, clammy.

'Write to me, will you?' said Des.

'OK.'

Des's pale, cold eyes looked at him pleadingly.

Ralph woke up in the night, thinking about him, and wondered.

> *Summer is gone*
> *October twilight*
> *Steals through my skylight*
> *And weaves its spell.*

> *I live again*
> *In dreams of springtime*
> *Our wedding ringtime*
> *When all was well.*

The soft, caressing voice of Archie Lewis, singing with the schmaltzy Geraldo Strings. Ralph lay listening contentedly. All was right with the world.

Instead of Des there was Tom, instead of Glyn there was Ed. Both were quiet, inoffensive, no older than himself.

He had been there for nearly a year and was resigned to his lot. This was his home, the San: long chicken-coop blocks laid out in parallel rows on the hillside, patients mooching along corridors in drab utility dressing-gowns, Olive Chips fluttering her hand on her way to the kitchens, Doctor John shyly enquiring: 'How are you feeling in yourself?'

And Sister O'Neill clasping the files hard to her tits.

This was his home, and the redbrick house by the river was impossibly remote. Dad going to work, Mam pegging clothes out on the line, Joe urging on the

Wanderers from the touchline: they belonged to a land of dreams barely worth thinking about.

He snuggled down closer under the bedclothes.

Two hearts were gay
Our yesterday
Seemed like a dream come true,
But summer has gone,
Gone with the song we knew.

Now in the pale
October twilight
I pray that you might
Remember too.

He thought of the girl, and the letter he should never have posted.

Autumn drifted into the ward, cool and earthy. Rafts of swallows swirled away south. At evening, the brightly-lit ward shut out the dark. Beyond the flung-open french windows the world stretched out to infinity, unknowing and unknowable.

He was getting better at making stuffed toys now. The fluffy kapok did not stick out between the stitches in such an unruly way as before, and the completed objects were more recognisable.

Some of the boys made money out of the things they made, but he didn't have the nerve. He simply gave them away to anyone who wanted them. One of them went to his baby niece Rosalind, another to the little girl who lived next door at home. He had a sudden wish to give one to Morwen Phillips, if she turned up again. If.

He made her bambi very carefully, cutting out the pattern far more meticulously than hitherto, pulling the stitches tight. He even managed the difficult piece around the head without making a mess of it. When he had finished, not a wisp of kapok showed through.

He held it in his hands, gazing at it admiringly.

'What the fuck's that?' asked Llew amiably.

'A bambi.'

'Looks more like a fucking dead donkey to me.'

Ralph put it carefully in his locker, proud of his success.

A letter came from Des on Hospital Block. The handwriting was cramped, almost illegible, sloping to the right with exaggerated masculinity. Ralph read it with a surprise that quickly turned to embarrassment. It was written in a childish, affectionate way, as if they had been bosom pals. Ralph put it aside, not wishing to read it again, ever. There was something disturbing about it, and Ralph realised what it was. Des had been fond of him. In spite of all the bullying, he had been fond of him. Was that the reason for the bullying? The staggering, sickening question bore down on him darkly.

Ralph tore the letter to shreds and put it in the waste-paper bin. He pulled the blankets over his head, trying to think of other things.

'How are you feeling in yourself?' asked Doctor John for the millionth time.

'Alright thank you, doctor,' replied Ralph automatically.

He waited for him to snap the file shut and hand it back to Sister O'Neill. But he didn't.

'Temperature alright these days, I see,' said Doctor John. 'Good, good.'

He looked at Ralph. 'We shan't be needing the PP. You're doing much better now.'

'Am I?' Ralph warmed to the praise and felt the first stirrings of hope.

'Your weight's not very good, though. Still only 7 stone 10.'

'I know,' admitted Ralph, ashamed of his shortcomings.

'You should try eating more,' said the doctor reproachfully. 'Is he eating well, Sister?'

'Not as well as he should,' said Sister O'Neill, blushing as she always did when he addressed her.

'You must try harder. We'd like to get you up but we can't yet.'

He paused, as if expecting some response.

'I'm sorry,' said Ralph inadequately.

'Tell you what,' said the doctor briskly. 'When you reach eight stone we'll put you on hours. What do you say, Sister?'

She nodded and smiled and took the file from him.

They went on their way, Doctor John with hands clasped behind his back, Sister O'Neill with rounded bum provocatively swaying.

They were weighed every three weeks in the doctor's room at the end of the corridor.

'Fill your pyjama pocket with money,' urged Llew. 'You'll get up to eight stone easy.'

He didn't want to do that, not because he was afraid of being found out but because he wouldn't really have earned it. He wanted to do things properly, not take the risk of a relapse. He was haunted by the picture of Bobby sitting up in bed, racked with coughs that tore his lungs apart. He'd grown so thin there was nothing of him. Mam had to put great wads of cotton wool under him, because of the bedsores.

'Well, drink plenty of water then before they weigh you. You'll put on a few pounds that way. Christ, do you want to stay in that bed for ever?'

Drinking water seemed okay. That was natural, wasn't it? He drank five or six tumblers full before the weigh-in. He felt bloated and nauseous.

As he stepped on the scales, he glanced guiltily at Sister O'Neill. She didn't even look at him.

'Seven stone 10,' she said impassively, noting it down in his file.

It hadn't made a blind bit of difference. That night he had the runs and his bowels were loose for days.

Ken Black came to visit. 'I'm thinking of going home,' he said nonchalantly.

'You can't do that!'

'Why not? I can get better just as well at home as I can here.'

'No you can't. That's stupid.'

'I don't think it means anything, all this treatment. It's just a way of getting rid of us.'

'What do you mean?'

'Well, if we're all in here together we can't infect anyone, can we?'

Ralph stared at him, remembering his fear of catching the bug off Bobby. He'd even avoided sitting with him. He was seized by the ghost of an old guilt.

'I think nature cures us, not the quacks,' said Ken. 'They may help it a bit, but not much.'

'I think you're wrong,' said Ralph vehemently. 'I think they help it a lot. If we stayed at home we'd die. Look what happened to Tarzan.'

Tarzan had died, after discharging himself from the San.

'We only hear about the bad cases,' said Ken, unimpressed. 'We don't hear about the ones that get better.'

Ralph looked across at Ronnie uneasily. He had his headphones on and didn't appear to be listening.

'You mustn't leave,' said Ralph. 'You'd be daft.'

Ken smiled. 'I don't suppose I will. But if I don't get hours soon, I'll seriously consider it. I don't want to end up with a long-service flag, like you.'

He took the tattered Union Jack from its socket, ran it lightly over Ralph's head, then put it back.

His mother came to visit, as promised. Her cheeks seemed rosier than ever. She brought him cakes and orange squash and a couple of books about cricket.

'How's Morwen?' he asked.

'Who?'

'Morwen at Cherry Farm. Where you're staying.'

'Oh, she's alright, bach. Didn't know who you meant for a minute. Don't see much of her—I don't interfere with the family.'

'She came to see me once, a few weeks back.'

'Did she? There's nice.'

'She didn't say anything, then?'

'No, I don't think so.' Mam looked at him shrewdly. 'Don't expect too much, son.'

'I don't,' he said, blushing. 'Just wondered, that's all.'

He knew she wanted to put her hands on his, but he kept them tight under the bedclothes. What did she think he was? He wasn't a kid any more.

She twisted her gnarled hands together.

All at once he wanted to go home. He saw the redbrick house by the river, the gulls wheeling and diving. He heard the shouts from Town Field when Aber were playing. He saw the kids playing in the street, his father dozing by the fire, Joe going out of an evening. He felt the wind on his face on the prom.

The bell rang to bring visiting to an end. His mother stood up and bent over to kiss him. He kissed her cheek quickly, then turned his head away.

'You're alright, aren't you, son?'

'Yes. I'm alright.'

'Sure now?'

'Course.'

'You'll be home soon. I know you will.'

Yes, he thought. Home in six months.

He said nothing.

The wheel of the seasons turned slowly, bringing its spokes back to the same positions as before. Mynydd

Troed put on its white cloak again. The carol singers hark-the-heralded and good-king-wenceslased on the verandah. Once more the wards were paper-chained and mistletoed.

He walked down to the Christmas concert with Ken Black, feeling the awkwardness of sportsjacket and grey flannels more acutely than ever after another year of bedrest. The show was much the same as before: in-jokes about the bug, some safe lampooning of popular members of staff, a daring shaft or two aimed at Jock, and a brutally satirical song about Doctor Kerrigan's legendary lack of finesse with refills:

> When she took away the needle, he went
> floating far away
> At Much-Binding-in-the-San!

The boys roared in male, jollyhockeysticks style. At the end they all gave three cheers for Jock. He rose, the old commandant, acknowledging the applause of his captives. Outside, the invisible guards circled the perimeter with their ghost-hounds, enslaving the boys with fear of the outside world, fear of death.

Des wrote again from Hospital Block, pleading for a visit from Ralph.

You can do it Ralphie boy, all you've got to do is hop along here when nobody's looking. I'm lonely as hell here, you don't see any bugger from morning till night. Think of the good times we had and come and see your old mate.

Ralph tore the letter up, feeling powerful and triumphant. Also, he recognised, he was taking pleasure in being cruel. The tables were turned and now, though in a more subtle way, he was the bully and Des the victim. He gloried in it, discovering more about himself every day.

His weight crept up to 7 stone 12, without the aid of pennies in his pyjama pocket or water in his gut. He was eating better and feeling stronger. His whole outlook was changing. He felt more confident, not only about his ability to get well but about the kind of person he was. His slow conquest of the bug went along with his increasing sense of being someone of value. If he had not stood up to Mel and Des, neither had he gone under. And both had recognised his status: Mel by giving him the flag, Des by writing him those pitiful letters.

January dropped away, as if it had never happened.

In February Doctor John said: 'When the weather gets better we'll put you on hours.'

By the third week winter had gone. He was allowed out of bed for an hour a day, then two, then four.

He sat in the dayroom on Block M, playing crib and reading the papers.

He got used to wearing clothes again.

He went visiting the boys in the other wards.

He was one of the élite.

7 Walking wounded

'Ready?' Philip asked. He loomed in the doorway of Ralph's cubicle, scrunching his walking stick impatiently into the tiled floor of the corridor.

'Just a minute.' Ralph, in sports jacket and baggy grey flannels, unlocked the beech-green door of the tall metal locker by his bed. He reached in, took out a shabby fawn raincoat.

'Not wearing that thing, are you?' said Philip, appalled.

'Yes. Why not?'

'It looks disgusting, that's why. I wouldn't be seen dead in it.'

'You won't be, don't worry.'

He put on the coat, did the belt up, looked defiant.

Philip shook his head. 'Don't know why I bother with you, honest to God I don't.'

'You needn't if you don't want to.'

'Don't know why you need it anyway,' grumbled Philip. 'It's not going to rain.'

'It might. Anyway it'll be cold walking.'

'Cold! You're too bloody thin, boy, that's your trouble.'

'Can't help that. Anyway I'm not as thin as I was.'

Philip sighed, started down the corridor. Ralph followed.

They stepped from Block G into the chill April air. Ralph breathed in deeply, exhilarated. The sensation of being fully clothed was still a novelty. Even to have shoes on seemed luxurious. He wrinkled his toes as he walked, self-indulgent as an old crone warming her shanks by the fire.

Philip was one of his new-found friends, now he had put bedrest behind him. He was like a big shaggy dog, black-haired, comfortable. He spoke a bit posh, having been a sixth-former in Monmouth School for Boys when snatched away by the bug. He never spoke of his family, but Ralph knew his father was a vet. He had seen him once, tall, straight-backed, distant in manner.

Ralph was still mildly surprised by his friendship; they had little in common. Philip didn't seem to read much; his interests were scientific. Socially he was a cut above the crowd; his conversation was startling for its almost complete absence of swearing. Neither had latched on to the other, but somehow they graduated to each other's company as if by some natural law. Ralph enjoyed being with him; even the fact that Philip said little was a bonus. Ralph had grown tired of the almost continual Block M fractiousness, born of frayed consumptive nerves and tired bodies. In contrast, Block G was restful. The boys all had their own cubicles (known, flatteringly, as 'chalets', as if imported from the Alps), which, although tiny, were given a degree of individual character. Ralph had a small bookcase, and a battery radio that picked up AFN—the American Forces Network. Nearly everyone on the block had one, but Philip wasn't interested. 'What do I want with that rubbish?' he said disdainfully. He listened to the Third Programme through the hospital headphones, while Ralph had his ear pressed to Tommy Dorsey and Charlie Barnet.

Walking at the prescribed steady pace, they made

their way along the covered way to the perimeter path that encircled the sanatorium. They were both on one-and-one; one circuit of the path in the morning, one in the afternoon. Some believed this totalled two miles, but Philip was derisive. 'Not even a mile altogether,' he scoffed.

Ralph protested; it must be more than that.

'Well, mile and a half then,' Philip conceded. 'If that,' he added sourly.

They joined the tramp around the circuit. Some went singly, others in twos or threes. The pace of the walkers varied; those on three-and-three went briskly, showing off their fitness. They brushed past the laggard one-and-ones like greyhounds derisive of lesser breeds. One or two of them, dandruff cases who had briefly favoured Block M with their presence, called out greetings to Ralph as they went by.

'Made it at last then? 'Bout time!'

'Go easy now, Ralph—don't start mopping, you bugger!'

'Where's the flag, Ralph—bring it with you?'

All was good humour; it was almost (but not quite) as though Des had never happened.

They still had to rest before meals for an hour. This was thought to improve the appetite; but Ralph's appetite was better than it had ever been, except in those long-lost days of infancy when Mam had been milky and warm and nothing bad could ever happen.

Rest Hour meant lying on your bed, fully clothed, reading or listening to the wireless.

Ralph loved his cell in Block G. He was free here, as he never had been before. No elder brothers and sisters to nag him; no school; no Block M forced matiness or bullying.

No fear of dying like Bobby, so long as his health kept improving.

He sighed with contentment, looking out at Mynydd Troed through the french windows. It seemed altogether friendlier from here, blushing fresh-green with the joys of spring.

The coils of worry that had clamped tight to his brain had gone now. Perhaps they would never come back; he willed them not to, tried to stop thinking about them in case the mere thinking might endanger him.

I'm getting better, he told himself fiercely. He remembered what his sister Gwen had taught him to say to himself, years before the bug had pursued him: 'Every day, and in every way, I am getting better and better.'

He repeated the words to himself, whispering them to the pillow.

Meals were eaten communally, the boys sitting at long trestle tables. They were loud, vulgar occasions, not for the squeamish. Sausages were 'widows' memories', fish dishes an excuse for coarse gynaecological comparisons. Supplies of food seemed inexhaustible. The boys were encouraged to eat, and some ate to excess. They had second helpings, or even third; Oliver Twist would have thought himself in Paradise. At breakfast one morning, the gross Arnold Gage consumed no fewer than thirteen kippers. He became a legend in his time, a monument to greed and opportunism.

Mental boundaries widened, as well as the physical. Ralph read the *News Chronicle* more acutely, beginning to feel a sense of being part of the world rather than observer of a distant pageant. War had broken out between North and South Korea, and there was talk of its spreading.

'This would have meant world war at one time,' one of the doctors said casually.

Ralph was shocked, that a person presumably dedicated to healing could be so indifferent to murder and suffering.

He knew he had much to learn in life, but did not like the learning. Much of his innocence had long gone out of the window, blown away by the rough realism of the San. He could talk now as dirty as any; knew that marriage vows were made to be broken; discovered that the milk of loving-kindness flowed thin as water. Yet his political idealism remained; he was Labour, believing in the Brotherhood of Man and the ultimate triumph of Socialism.

He did not yet think much of what he might do when released. To get out was still the overriding purpose in life, the great prize that might yet be snatched away by a Relapse.

The word was a horror, haunting the imagination.

In his growing strength and vitality, Ralph found great satisfaction. He woke early, suffused by a sense of well-being. His cubicle was as wide open to the weather as Ward 8 had been in Block M, but the very air seemed different. In a crude sense it was, since Block G was too far from the kitchen to be affected by the contagion of early morning haddock. But in a subtle way too it was cleaner, more health-giving, as it seemed to come from the great world beyond the prison gates of the sanatorium. Washing in the dubs he sang the popular songs of the day. When told to pipe down or shut that fucking row up, he answered in kind. For the first time in years, possibly the first time ever, he was at ease with himself, standing on the brink of a manhood that held unlimited potential. He felt he could be anything he wanted to be, so long as he didn't slide back into the pit.

Away from the bedrest restrictions of Block M, his circle of friends grew wider; so, too, did his knowledge of human types. Apart from the quiet, stolid Philip there was Dai Check, squat, blackhaired, Neanderthal; Tony Ledger, tall, floppy-Saxon-haired, aesthetic; Donald John, eager, questing, optimistic; Bryan Eagle, irredeemably cynical; Rodney Paul, dark-eyed, probing, a man of gallows humour, not to be trusted.

Ralph could cope with them all. No longer the sickly, spewing greenhorn of eighteen months ago, he knew a bit about life now. Nobody would bully him again; and Des could die, the bastard.

One round in the morning, one in the afternoon. Two rounds in the morning, one in the afternoon. Two rounds in the morning, two in the afternoon. One and one, two and one, two and two.

He saw the starry celandine, felt the wind on his face. With May came the froth of pink and white blossom, the cuckoo chiming from the woods behind the nurses' home. He exulted in everything but became restive with

Philip's company. It seemed to him that the vet's son knew everything about the countryside, but saw nothing. He knew the names of trees, birds, plants, but saw not their beauty or meaning. Worst of all he felt nothing; not the sap in the branch nor the spring in the stem. Nor, crucially, the fear in the hunted fox.

'We've got to have hunting to keep the numbers down,' he argued, stoically planting one foot ahead of the other.

'There must be other ways. Anyway, what harm do foxes do?'

A slow, indulgent smile. 'You ever seen a lamb with its throat torn out by a fox, Ralph? Not a pretty sight, believe me.'

'Well, you could shoot them. Or gas them.'

Philip stopped. 'You think that's less cruel than hunting? You don't know what you're talking about, boy.'

'But it's horrible, obscene! Think what the fox *feels*—being hunted.'

'I don't know they feel anything,' Philip said, plodding on. 'It's part of nature. They may even enjoy it.'

'Enjoy it! Would you?'

Philip chuckled. 'I'm not a fox.'

Lying awake at night, clamped headphones shutting out owl cries and wind sighs, Ralph listened to AFN and dreamed. He was lead trumpet in a swing band, standing up to play fantastic solos, his gleaming horn catching the light as his golden notes shimmered through the dance hall. Everyone stopped dancing to stare at him in wonder, applauding wildly when he sat down. The bandleader smiled at him, the band pounded out a riff in which his trumpet scaled dizzy heights to the spectacular climax. Suddenly the scene changed and they were in his old school, playing in the assembly hall with the kids sitting there amazed. He was a success at last, not a sick absentee. The kids who'd forgotten all about him remembered him again, pointing at him in wonder and clapping like fun. Then, the music done, they crowded round him, slapping his back, demanding his autograph.

He fell asleep in the middle of his fantasies.

In the morning he knew he would never set foot in that school again as long as he lived.

Every Monday morning he stood before Jock the Medical Superintendent, to be told if he were advancing, standing still or retreating. All the élite, the walking wounded, had to endure this. It was a measure of their status that their progress, or regression, was measured by the Boss himself, not a subordinate doctor doing the rounds of the bedridden.

Jock had a tough, close-cropped skull, the kind called bullet-headed in adventure stories. He was a four-square, pugnacious man, dictatorial and unbending. His manner towards his patients was that of a squire to the peasantry, veering between the patronising and the disdainful.

'What happens if you leave your tools out in the rain?' he asked someone who had been careless with a pair of Sanatorium-issue shears.

'They go rusty, sir,' came the cringing reply.

'Well, don't let it happen again.'

To call Jock 'sir' was commonplace. His appearance seemed to demand it. He wore a country gentleman's tweed suit, a cut above the white coats of the other doctors and Sister McGaw's stiff blue uniform. She cast disapproving looks at all who entered the inner sanctum, endorsing the great man's pronouncements with slight nods or shakes of the head.

Ralph held Jock in some awe, but managed to avoid calling him 'sir.' It reminded him of the school he had left behind and of the National Service he was now certain to miss. There was, too, a strain of stroppiness in his nature which was gaining strength as his health improved, an inheritance from the Cardiganshire peasants on his father's side of the family.

Having advanced to three rounds of the perimeter path in the morning and three in the afternoon, he now stood on the brink of the physical tasks known as 'the grades', designed (officially) as a means of testing the patient's strength before discharge or (unofficially) as cheap labour.

Jock scowled down at Ralph's file, handed to him by Sister McGaw. Viewed from above, the short spikes of his iron-grey crop looked razor-sharp.

'You've been managing the rounds alright?' he asked curtly.

'Yes thank you.'

'No tiredness?'

'No.'

'None at all?' Jock's head jerked up; his cold eyes met Ralph's, defying him to lie.

'Well,' faltered Ralph, 'only sometimes.'

'Ah,' Jock lethally murmured. 'Sometimes.' He looked down again complacently. A thrill of mutual satisfaction seemed to pass between Sister McGaw and himself.

Ralph's knees weakened. He knew he'd be back now to two and two; or worse.

'Well,' said Jock, with steely good humour, 'it's only to be expected.'

With a flourish, he made a note in Ralph's file.

'You can begin the grades today,' he said. 'Get some grass cutters from Mr Smythe. He'll tell you where to go.'

Ralph was filled with elation. He had made it at last to the grades—after eighteen months he had made it! He looked gratefully at his benefactor, who had so unexpectedly favoured him.

'Thank you, sir,' he said humbly.

Smythe was a small, sour man in charge of the gardening tools at the San. Unlike George the Greek in the sub-post-office and Walter the librarian, he had never been a patient there. He had lived all his life in the village, a short distance from the sanatorium gates. He seemed to dislike all the inmates, squinting at them resentfully as he handed out the tools and took them back in again at the end of the day. He it was who had shopped the man who had dared to allow his shears to rust. Unquestionably, he was on the side of authority, opposed to the slackness and rebelliousness of the diseased.

He stared balefully as a smiling Ralph advanced on his wooden shack. 'Could you give me some shears please? Jock's just put me on grades.'

'Who?' he returned belligerently.

'Jock. Dr Maxwell.'

'That's better. Show some respect. New here, aren't you?'

'I've been here eighteen months,' said Ralph spiritedly.

'New to the grades, I mean. First day on them, is it?'

'Yes.'

'Well, make sure you do the work properly. Too many half-assed bastards messing things up here.'

'Give us a chance. I haven't even started yet.'

'Lot to say for yourself, haven't you? What's your name?'

'Ralph. Ralph Lloyd.'

'Well, *Mr* Lloyd, I'll be looking out for you. You ever used one of these before?'

'No.'

'Easy as winking. Only make sure you bring it back at four o'clock, right?'

'Course.'

With another hard stare, Smythe ducked under his counter. 'Here,' he said, with a jerk of the head.

He stood on the grass verge outside the hut, the long-handled shears pointing down to his boots. 'Stand straight, like this. Then—' He drew the handles apart then brought them smartly together, neatly clipping the grass border. 'You see?' Ralph nodded. 'And make sure you do it tidy. Not like an apeman's haircut.'

He told Ralph where to go. Ralph went on his way, whistling.

8 Eating Out

His letters home changed. He had never let on about his misery, but now his tone became more buoyant. His father responded in kind. Ralph felt the beginnings of a new relationship with him.

On Sunday morning the boys on grades were allowed a great adventure: breakfast at Cherry Farm in the village.

'Ham and eggs! Lovely, mun. Never tasted anything like it.'

They togged up in smart jackets and ties and trooped down the steep back lane known as Haemorrhage Hill, a name that did not appear on any map but was even used by the locals. Dubbed this by some black humorist in the San long ago, it was said to be the ultimate test for weak lungs.

Ralph was reluctant to go because it might mean meeting Morwen, whose visit to Block M he had handled so badly. Thinking about it, he blushed. She had not come back to see him again, and no wonder.

It was Philip who persuaded him to go. 'What's the point of hanging round up here? May as well see a bit of life.'

He fumbled awkwardly with his walking stick, poking his turn-ups with it aimlessly. He avoided Ralph's eye; Ralph felt a stab of guilt, at having distanced himself from him since the contretemps over fox hunting. Of course Philip was wrong about that; but there was so much right about him. Ralph was amazed by how far he had come in a short time. A few months ago, when being bullied by

Des, he would have been glad of a kind word from anyone. Now here he was, rejecting a friendship freely offered!

'Alright,' he said impulsively. 'I'll come with you.'

'Good lad.' Philip smiled back gratefully. For the first time Ralph realised that, for no clearly understood reason, he could be important to someone.

Philip clumped down the hill beside him, his brightly polished boots sounding charged and confident. Ralph stole a glance at him; his round, boyish face spoke of the openness of the countryside, a sense of ease with the roughness of nature that he, a town boy, would never match. It occurred to him that, were it not for the bug, he would never have been friends with anyone like this. The San was a melting pot, into which all human varieties were thrown.

It was worth going to Cherry Farm, just for the walk down Haemorrhage Hill. The narrow country lane, framed by hedges and tall trees, seemed to enclose all the sap and thrust of spring in its narrow compass. Smells of earth and all things growing, drawn out by the sun, blended into a diffuse atmosphere, subtle and intoxicating. Ralph breathed of it deeply, cleansing his lungs of disease. He felt young, vital, renewed.

He entered Cherry Farm, two strides behind Philip, with a self-confidence he had never known before. Faces looked up at him, many smiling, from people who knew him by sight if not by name. A thrill of gratitude ran through him. He felt one of the crowd, something he had never felt at school. He paused, not knowing which way to go, then saw Philip waving him to a place at his table. He edged his way there, returning smiles and greetings.

'First time out, Ralph? Good boy!'

'Hi, Ralph! Put some flesh on you, this will!'

'Put lead in his pencil!' Bellows of laughter, an outpouring of male cameraderie. Ralph burst with pride; he had no idea he was so popular.

There were two others at the table besides Philip and himself: Tony Ledger, tall, floppy-Saxon-haired, and Llew, dark, ex-Ward 9, who had taken control when Ronnie flipped, threatening to go home.

'What are you doing here?' Ralph asked Llew unthinkingly, still hot with success. 'You're not on grades yet, are you?'

'Pipe down, you daft bugger,' Llew muttered. 'Don't want me slung out, do you?'

'Oh. Sorry.'

Tony, face turned away, pretended not to hear. He had his elbows on the white tablecloth, arms upright, the ends of his long tapering fingers tapping one another lightly. Philip grinned.

'He needs looking after, Llew. Can't take him anywhere.'

'That's obvious.' But Llew was smiling; he had been forgiven.

'What block you on now then, Llew?' asked Ralph, keen to make amends.

'J. With the pensioners. Nobody there under forty. You're on G I suppose, aren't you?'

'Yes.'

'Wish I was young enough to be there with you, *myn uffern i*. They're a dull bloody lot where I am.'

Llew, nasal-toned, was a railwayman from Corwen; a dandruff case through and through.

'Funny how they divide us up by age,' mused Philip. 'Think we'd be all the same, wouldn't you?'

'All the same inside, at any rate,' said Llew. 'Rotten to the core.'

'Don't say that,' Ralph began, but was interrupted by Tony.

'I suppose it's community of interests they go by,' he said carefully. 'They think people the same age have more in common.'

Philip and Llew gave each other a glance; a low-brow confederacy against anything vaguely intellectual.

Ralph looked down, wanting to say something but tongue-tied. Tony, absorbed in thought, seemed oblivious to the sudden silence.

'Well,' said Llew, rough-voiced. 'Here's the sodding ham and eggs anyway. Grub up, Ralph. Get it down you.'

He had half expected Morwen to bring the food to the table, but there was no sign of her. He felt at once relieved and disappointed, realising for the first time how much he had been looking forward to seeing her again. He wanted to make amends to her: not by apologising (that would be too crass and embarrassing) but by being more natural and friendly with her than he had been that day she had visited him, both of them tongue-tied and awkward.

He looked around as he ate, taking in the mellowness and age of the room where they were munching.

Something of the atmosphere of old times lingered there, giving the room a restfulness which acted as a balm on the spirits. The mood was relaxed, the banter more subdued than in the febrile air of the sanatorium. The slow pendulum of a grandfather clock measured time in long moments. A dark-wooded dresser, clasped with cups and bearing dishes that had come from the kiln a century ago, stood expansively nearby. Ralph suddenly felt an intruder: this was Morwen's home, a place full of shades of her ancestors. And suddenly he glimpsed her, through the door leading to the kitchen. Their eyes met: he imagined she blushed. A strange sensation, both pleasurable and perplexing, seized his stomach. Nobody noticed a thing. When he looked up next, she had gone.

He still had refills for his AP every week, only now they were performed by Dr Lang, in whose domain Block G lay. Brisker and older than Dr John, he had a weathered face and stubby fingers. They expertly jiggled the bottles that controlled the pressure of air through the pleural wall, that kept the lung collapsed. Ralph lay on his left side, right hand hooked behind his head, leaving room for the needle to be jabbed into his side. He was as trusting as ever, as little capable of questioning the wisdom of the San as of defying gravity. The rules and rigours of the regime were Holy Writ; were they not so, what was he doing there?

Dr Lang wrenched the needle out more roughly than Dr John. The nurse dabbed his punctured skin with a swab, and smiled. He clambered down from the high couch and put his shirt back on; the doctor was preoccupied, already looking at the next patient's file.

'How long will it be now, do you think?' asked Ralph suddenly.

'Eh?'

'Before I go home. How long, do you think?'

Dr Lang frowned. 'That depends on a lot of things. You've only just got on the grades, haven't you?'

'Yes, but—I'd like to know.'

'Impossible to say, laddie.' Lang's lowlands Scottish accent jangled Ralph's nerves. 'Just carry on as you are.'

'But if I keep doing alright,' Ralph persisted, 'd'you think I'll be home for Christmas?'

He almost saw the words 'which Christmas?' framed on Lang's lips, but the words that came out were, 'You might be. We'll have to wait and see.'

'I'll have been here over two years by then. I can't stay here for ever.' Ralph, disgusted with himself, heard his voice rise to an almost feminine pitch.

'Who says we want you to? There are plenty outside waiting to come in, laddie.'

Ralph fumbled with his shirt cuff, struggling to do it up. His eyes prickled with tears of anger. The nurse fiddled with the instruments by the AP appliance, pretending nothing was happening.

'I know it's hard,' said Lang, softening. 'But we want to do the job properly. You wouldn't want to go home and have to come back again, would you?'

Ralph shook his head, not trusting himself to speak.

'You're doing alright. Your AP's taken well. Keep on as you are and there's every hope. But I can't make any promises. Understand?'

Ralph nodded. He snatched up his jacket and tie and strode out. He blinked on the concrete causeway, stupefied by the strangeness of his feelings. Then he hurried back to the safety of Block G and flung himself full-length on the bed. His side ached as it had never done before.

'You see, Ralph,' said Philip sombrely, 'it's all a matter of getting things in proportion.'

His trowel scuffed the soil. Expertly he lifted a weed and put it in the basket beside him, where he knelt by the flower bed.

'It seems a long time in here,' he went on. 'But it's nothing really, in a lifetime.'

His dark, dusty face was shaded by the floppy white sanatorium-issue hat he had pulled low over his brow to keep the hot sun from his eyes. 'Is it now?' he persisted.

He gave Ralph a keen look, having something in it of the natural sense of superiority of the twenty-year-old over the seventeen-year-old.

'You're talking like a bloody visitor,' said Ralph, attacking a weed viciously with his trowel.

'Now come on, Ralph.' Philip smiled patronisingly. 'You can't get away with that. You know as well as I do—'

'I'm sick of this place—sick of it!' His trowel skewed around, stabbing a flower stem cruelly.

'Hey—careful there! You're supposed to be weeding, not murdering the buggers.'

'I don't care. It's all cheap labour anyway, this. We shouldn't be doing it.'

'Who told you that, Ralph?'

'Llew.'

'Oh. Him. The railwayman from North Wales.' Philip resumed his careful sifting of the soil he loved, every grain and particle of it.

'It's true though, isn't it? We're robbing people of jobs, doing all this gardening.'

Philip paused, wiped his brow with a large blue handkerchief. 'You don't want to listen to talk like that. It's all Socialist rubbish.'

'I *am* a socialist.'

Philip smiled. 'You'll learn, boy. You'll learn.'

Placidly he worked on. Ralph straightened his back, hating him. He wanted to hit Philip with the trowel, see his blood drip into the scorched red soil.

The scuffing of Philip's trowel was the only sound in the still midsummer afternoon.

Ralph stared at Philip's broad back. All the anger drained from him, leaving him dazed and listless. He sighed, bent again to the task.

Sex (or the lack of it) was a constant problem. On Block M the sight of Sister O'Neill's swelling breasts beneath her crisp, virtuous uniform had always been stimulating but now, more than ever, the female form taunted and tantalised him. It did not have to be conventionally pretty to rouse him. A plump domestic he occasionally encountered would set his hands itching to fondle her big tits and fleshy legs. He longed to encircle her broad waist with his arms and press his hard cock against her. She smiled at him, he smiled back, and they passed one another. He wondered if magnetic waves from him penetrated her consciousness or if she were wholly indifferent to his lust.

Often the visions were inward, not outward. At night, listening on his headphones to the big bands and sentimental crooners, he dreamed up women clad in wispy, gossamer-thin gauzes, too insubstantial to be called clothing. Their nipples were misty-pink pleasure-cusps either side of their deep, shadowy clefts, their thighs lusciously curved beneath swelling hips and tight waists. His cock pushed up hard against the white sheet, the blankets thrown back on warm, oppressive nights. It throbbed with useless intent, longing for the grasp of a quim. Sometimes his hand clutched it, just to feel the reciprocal heat of hand and cock, one feeding the other. But his hand did nothing more and, the contact lost, his cock, denied relief, at last shrank back, dry and defeated. Some boys wanked and some refrained; no one knew who did or who didn't. All suffered, their adolescence wasting away.

He was reluctant to go back to Cherry Farm next Sunday morning, fearing Morwen's scorn. After breakfast in the dining hall he walked down the drive and out of the main gates, turning right away from the village. He was becoming used to the sight of traffic now, though there was little enough of it in the Breconshire countryside. They were allowed these short walks outside the San on Saturdays and Sundays: a privilege of the élite. The long months when, fretful and ill, he had lain in bed on Block M, were already beginning to seem comfortably distant. He smiled indulgently, remembering his naïvete that first day, when he had actually told Mel he might be out in six months. Good old Mel; he hadn't been so bad after all. But his hatred of Des never abated. Another letter had come from Hospital Block, a frankly pathetic letter full of pitiful pleading. 'They've got me on blocks and I can't see a fucking thing out of the window. Please come and see me old son, I miss you like hell.' It was given him by George the Greek, who looked at him with large reproachful eyes. 'Thanks,' said Ralph brusquely, seeing the writing on the envelope. He read it quickly then tore it up, putting the bits in a waste bin. He would never go near Des; never go near Hospital Block; it was a place of the defiled, and he would have none of it.

He branched right from the main road, into a lane he had never entered before. It sloped slightly downhill, into a hollow where the branches of the elms interlaced overhead. Sunlight filtered through the leaves, casting a green, liquid light into this natural tunnel. All was cool, earthy and calm. A ditch beside the high bank had almost dried in the heat, its dark, musty smell mingling with the lighter fragrance of the hedgerow flowers. Ralph stood still, awestruck by such beauty. Then he heard footsteps. He had an impulse to flee human company. Walking on, steeling himself for the encounter, he turned a bend and saw Morwen briskly approaching.

Seeing him, she slackened pace momentarily. She had on a white blouse and dark blue skirt which had a tapering effect, emphasising her slimness. Her black hair, caught by the dappled sunlight, seemed to have a sheen to it, as if soaked in liquid gold. He was afraid she might walk right past without looking at him; he wasn't sure at which precise moment he should try to meet her eye and greet her. The problem, though it only occupied a few seconds, troubled him. He looked up, too soon, cast his eyes down, looked up again. She met his eyes gravely.

'Hullo,' he said, the colour rising to his cheeks. 'Fancy seeing you here.'

She half-smiled, nonplussed, and he ploughed on stupidly, 'You're out early, aren't you?'

'I've been to my auntie's. How long you been up and about then?' she asked brightly.

'Oh, a few months now. I'm on grades.'

'That's nice. I expect you'll be going home soon then.'

'Not really. I'm only on grade one.'

'Oh, are you?' she said vaguely, and again he felt foolish. Why should she be interested in the grades?

Her voice was lower in pitch than he remembered it, more musical. Her face had filled out a little; and so had her breasts.

'What you got there then—been picking flowers, have you?' he asked, with a jocularity which sounded, to his own ears, forced and ridiculous.

'Yes. Just a few for my mother,' she replied, glancing down at the small hedgerow posy she had gathered.

He almost blundered into another quasi-humorous remark about the heinousness of picking wild flowers, but checked himself just in time. 'They look nice,' he said.

'She loves flowers—wild ones best.'

'My mother's the same.'

'Is she?'

He became tongue-tied, remembering their stilted conversation in Ward 8, all those months ago.

'Why are you on your own?' she asked curiously. 'Haven't you got any friends?'

'Of course I have, but—' He thought of them guzzling ham and eggs in Cherry Farm at that moment. 'I like being on my own sometimes,' he added lamely.

'Well . . .' She hesitated. 'Better be getting along now. Enjoy your walk.'

'Don't go yet,' he said, surprising himself.

'I must—Mam's expecting me.'

She began to pass in a wider arc than necessary, her eyes averted.

'When can I see you again?'

She paused, surprised. 'I don't know.'

'What about one night in the week?'

'You're not allowed out then, are you?'

'I could make it. Just for an hour or so.'

She shrugged. 'I don't mind. But I don't want you to get into trouble for me.'

'I won't, don't worry.' His heart raced. 'What about Tuesday?'

She frowned, shook her head.

'Wednesday then. Right?'

'I don't know.'

'Please. Morwen.'

The use of her name made her glance at him quickly. 'Alright then. But don't blame me if—'

'Where shall I see you?' he asked breathlessly. 'Top of Haemorrhage Hill?'

She shook her head. 'No. Come to the house. I'll wait for you there.' She began walking away quickly, as if already regretting the commitment.

'What time—half-past seven?'

'If you like.'

The words wafted up into the overhanging boughs, setting up a strange rustling, as if the planned illicit meeting was already sending out shock waves.

9 Breaking Bounds

There was a letter from Billy next day, the first for many months.

Dear Ralph,

Just thought I'd drop you a line to hope your getting on OK. I saw your father in town the other day and he said you were up and about now. About time too! I expect you'll be home for next football season now. I played for Penparcau last season. We got to the semi-final of the cup and then lost to Rovers. I scored our only goal. I don't know if I should say this but Betty Pratt's going out with Neil Andrews, that slob from South Wales who thinks he sings like Bing Crosby. She put her nose up in the air when she saw me, she's really stuck up now. Youve had a lucky escape.

Well I must close now so thats it. Keep up the good work. Your old pal Billy.

Ralph smiled, folded the letter, put it in his locker with the others from Billy.

He went before Jock again that morning and was told to carry on with the same job as last week. He looked down at Jock's stubby grey hairs and thought, if only you knew. I am about to break the San's rules. I am going out of the grounds on a Wednesday evening. I should be worried as hell. But I'm not.

He felt much older and wiser. A burden had been lifted from him. All his life till now he had done things by the rules. But now he was breaking them.

He took stock of himself. In three months' time he'd be eighteen. Old enough to fight in a war and die in battle. Not old enough to vote. But old enough to get married and have children.

He began to see the months spent on bedrest as a watershed between childhood and adulthood. If he'd still been in Ward 8 on Block M nothing much would have changed. He would still be locked in his childhood, a prey to worry and bullying. But now all that was behind him. He was beginning to cope with life.

When he had asked Morwen out, in that moment of desperation, he had thought she'd refuse. Her acceptance changed everything. He was someone to reckon with. He felt ten years older.

She answered the door almost at once, then closed it quickly behind her. She gave him a shy, nervous glance, almost as though she were surprised to see him. After the initial greeting neither spoke a word as they walked along the short path to the iron gate he had left open. It squeaked as she shut it.

He smiled. 'Which way?'

'Any way you like,' she said impatiently.

'Let's go along the lane—where we were the other day.'

'OK.'

He realised, too late, that this meant walking past the sanatorium gates. He had planned to go the other way, past the bottom of Haemorrhage Hill! It was her impatient tone of voice that had done it; he had lost his grip for a second. Well, there was nothing for it now but to go on. He prayed they wouldn't meet any of the staff coming in or going out; what if Jock himself should appear? He'd be thrown out, no messing. Some minor rules you could break, without too much trouble; this was a major one, cast in stone.

The heatwave was over; it had ended the day before, with thunderclaps and jagged rain squeezing exquisite smells from the soil. The boys on grades had knocked off early, whooping and laughing. Ralph had stood in his chalet miserably, staring out at the rain, fearful it might last all next day, putting his date at risk. But, the storm over, the weather had brightened. The new day was mild, unassuming, the high white clouds drifting aimlessly by, the grass a fresher green for its dousing. Ralph, given another week's weeding by Jock, had worked mostly on his own, easing up the rogue plants with his trowel, filling his basket with them. His mind had been always on his meeting with Morwen. Now here she was, walking beside him in silence; already regretting she had let herself in for this, perhaps?

He knew he had to say something; anything.

'What you been doing today?' he asked. 'Much?'

'The usual. We've got exams coming up soon. I've been swotting, most of the time.'

It came as a surprise to realise she was still at school. 'What subjects?' he asked airily.

'History mainly. I hate it.'

'I know what you mean. All boring dates and things.'

He recalled his history master dictating notes in a droning voice; flying into sudden rages, then lapsing again into robotic mood.

'What do you really like?' he asked.

'Nothing really. I'm going to leave soon as I've done Higher. I'm only doing that 'cos Dad says I've got to.'

He had hardly ever seen her father, even when staying at the farm with his mother to visit big-brother Joe. Mr Phillips had been an occasionally-glimpsed figure, clumping about the yard in heavy boots or heard talking in the out-of-bounds kitchen, the words indistinguishable.

'Where'd you go to school then?'

'Brecon.'

'Go in on the bus, I suppose.'

'Mm-hm.'

'How long's it take you?'

'Oh, not long. Half an hour.'

They were within sight of the gates now. Ralph felt weak, his pulse quickening. Almost he wished himself back in the safety of his chalet, amid the easy cameraderie of the boys. The stupid worry he had felt over the girl writing to him on Block M returned as a pressure point on the back of his scalp. Why was he bothering with Morwen, before he was really cured? The sheen of the dark green laurel bushes at the bottom of the drive seemed suddenly menacing; it had a poisonous, rancorous look about it. He felt out of place, pitiable; she *forced* me into this, he thought wildly. They walked in silence past the gates; the long drive curved up to the distant chalets, uninhabited. Suddenly she stopped.

'Are you sure you want to do this?' she asked. 'I can easily go home, you know. It's no odds to me.'

Something in him wanted to say, 'Alright then,' taking the easy way out. But one glance at her steadied him. The proud tilt of her chin, the question in her dark eyes posed challenges to which his soul responded.

'Don't be silly. Of course I do.'

She relaxed perceptibly. He felt the warmth of triumph, as he had that first time he had stood up to Des on the day of Morwen's visit. They walked on, turning right into the lane where he had met her the previous Saturday. The shadows beneath the trees were deeper now as the sun tilted down the evening sky. Water gurgled in the ditch, fed by yesterday's storm. The smell and feel of the place were subtly different from before. Walking through the green tunnel between the elms, they drew instinctively closer. By accident, their hands touched. Ralph shivered, with the surprise of it. He did nothing at first, then clutched her hand clumsily. She let it lie within his, neither encouraging nor dissuading. He laced his fingers in hers, their palms touching. The feel of her arm against his, the clasping of their hands, filled him with a delight he had never experienced before.

'It was nice of you to call and see me—when I was still on bedrest.'

'That's OK . . . I should have come again, but I wasn't sure.'

'About what?' he asked, after a moment.

'If you wanted me to.'

He blushed, remembering how pathetic he had been.

'I don't blame you,' he said quietly. 'Anyway, I didn't expect you to. It's too much of a risk, isn't it?'

She glanced at him enquiringly.

'TB's catching,' he said. 'As if you didn't know.'

'Oh, we're used to it round here. We don't think about that much. Except . . .'

'Yes?'

'Oh, nothing.'

He was sure it wasn't nothing; that she had pulled back on the brink of an important revelation.

'You don't mind us all going down there on a Sunday morning? You aren't afraid of getting it yourself?'

'Why should I be? You're not infectious when they let you out, are you?'

'No, of course not,' he said quickly, although he was none too sure of that. 'But you might have different ideas.'

'If you're going to get it, you'll get it. That's what I think anyway.'

Ralph was silent, remembering his brother Bobby calling down from the bedroom, asking him to come up and keep him company, remembering too his reply: 'I can't. I'm doing my homework.'

But he had been lying, for the only reason he had not sat with Bobby was that he had been scared of catching the bug off him.

They were beginning to climb the rise on the far side of the tree-tunnel. It was only a gentle climb, but his heart began to pound and he felt a little breathless. He tried not to show it but had to stop, saying, 'Sorry. Just a sec.'

'You alright?' she asked anxiously.

'Yes. Fine.' He breathed deeply, feeling stupid. He did not want her to think him ill; she might be scared to be with him. They were standing very close; his upper arm touched her side, close by her breast.

Her eyes were full of concern, and something else. But he could do nothing, as yet.

'There. That's better.' He smiled, and resumed walking.

'We'll go back if you like.'

'No, not yet. Just a little bit further.'

They walked slowly uphill. He was acutely aware of their legs keeping pace with each other. One . . . two . . . Her hand had tightened its grip on his.

'How long have you been in there now, Ralph?' she asked gently.

'Twenty months.' He could almost quote the precise number of days.

'That's an awful long time. Haven't you felt like going home?'

'Yes, a lot. But I'm not going to, till I'm better.'

'I don't think I could. Stay in hospital that long, I mean.'

'You would if you had to.'

'Oh, I don't know. I wouldn't have the patience.'

Their pace slowed still further, even though they had now reached the brow of the hill.

'What are you going to do when you get out?' she asked in a soft, fluttering way.

'I don't know yet. I . . .'

He stopped, facing her. Her eyes darkened. He made to kiss her but she turned her head slightly so that his lips met her cheek. He held her tightly and tried again.

'Please, Ralph,' she gasped, and it was not clear to him whether this spelt rejection or acceptance.

This time he kissed the corner of her mouth. She made the slightest of efforts to push him away, then succumbed. Her lips were tightly closed, like those of the first girl he had kissed. She puckered them up in a shrinking, childish way which surprised him and filled him with sudden confidence. No longer was he afraid of her, or of what he might say. He realised that he knew much more than her about sexual matters, not from experience but through the corrupting, dirty talk in the San. Inhibited though it was, her kiss acted on his starved senses like an intoxicant. He squirmed his lips against hers, trying to relax them. She held them stiffly, then suddenly—through a convulsion in both their natures —their mouths were open and he felt the softness on the inside of her lips. She made a strange sound, half sigh, half groan, and he ran the fingers of his right hand down her spine, then lightly back up again. She tried to wriggle away but he held her close, his hardness forced against her through their clothing. An electric jolt stunned them: their tongues meeting. Uttering another half-articulate sound she shoved him away and stared at him, panting.

'What are you doing?' she asked wildly.

He took a step towards her but suddenly she started running. He grabbed at her as she passed but she threw him off easily. 'Morwen!' he called after her. 'Please! Stop! Morwen!' She whirled down the hill and around the bend at the bottom, her white legs like those of an animal at bay. Not once did she look back, though with all his strength he willed her to do so. He groaned.

He had mucked it up, good and proper. She would never see him again now. She might even report him to Jock.

He trudged down the hill miserably.

10 Double Top

'Where'd you get to last night?' asked Philip pugnaciously. 'I was looking everywhere for you.'

'I was up Block M, seeing some of my old mates.'

'Were you now?' He stood at the entrance to Ralph's cubicle, looking at him suspiciously. 'Don't know whether to believe you or not.'

'Why shouldn't you?' Ralph, making his bed, boldly looked back at Philip. He felt renewed confidence with morning, proud now that he had gone so far with Morwen, hopeful of persuading her out again.

'Dunno. You're a mystery to me, boy. You've changed so much.'

'In what way?'

Philip paused before answering, 'Too chopsy, that's your trouble. Come on, or we'll miss breakfast.'

The day ground slowly by. He was hoeing now, dragging the blunt wedge of the hoe along the plum-coloured Breconshire soil. The rows of runner beans climbed their wigwam-shaped poles. On one side the ground sloped away towards the main road, the shoe-shaped Mynydd Troed etched above the distant fields, while on the other the kitchen gardens rose to a sweep of unkempt grass hemmed in by the hedge bordering Haemorrhage Hill. The day was cool, the sunshine glinting palely through vapoury clouds, but all the boys wore their soft white hats as they went about their tasks, lest the sun-god should break free of its restraint and do their weak lungs damage. They wore old shirts with

114

sleeves rolled high, flannel trousers or corduroys, and their tanned skins belied the fragility of their health. They had not quite beaten the bug but held it at bay, as their lungs slowly healed and their bodies stiffened their resistance. Yet every month, two or three of the boys—sometimes more—tumbled back to bedrest to fight the war in the trenches all over again. Even those on sixth grade, with a possible date for release burnt into their brains, could succumb. It was all a lottery, decided by a fate more malicious than benign.

All Ralph's thoughts were on Morwen. Her voice tantalised him, saying, 'If you're going to get it, you'll get it. That's what I think anyway.' He felt the touch of her palm, the softness of her arm against his. Then the shock of their tongues meeting, the electric thrill of it. He paused, plunging the hoe into the ground, resting some of his weight against it. The other boys, spread out over the sanatorium grounds, seemed as dream figures, their soft hats bobbing up and down. What was he doing here? Suddenly he seemed to have no past and no future. The house in the redbrick row by the river belonged to another life, another person. He had been born here, a child of the bug, and when he left—if he left—he would become someone new entirely. Slowly he became suffused with a sense of well-being he had never known before. He felt free, absolved of all responsibility. This was why they stayed on here, he realised, Walter and George and others, doing menial tasks simply in order to avoid leaving. Why should they go? Where would they go to? This was a world apart, a refuge. Almost he felt he could stay here himself, for ever.

Then he remembered his mother, pegging the clothes out in the garden; and Joe, going to work; and his father.

He sighed heavily. The hoe, scrabbling between the rows of beans again, clunked dully against a stone.

The summer fete came that Saturday. Authority shone with benevolence. The medicos turned out in smart lightweight suits, all smiles and encouragement. Even Jock left his lair, to appear in all his squirearchical splendour. He did not deign to throw a rubber ball into a bucket, or to guess the number of peas in a bottle, but stood regally, hands neatly tucked into the pockets of his Harris tweed jacket (thumbs carefully hitched over the top), silently approving such frivolities. Visitors were smiled at, indulged. Patients were on their best behaviour. Nothing indecorous must happen, for this was the one day in the year when the San opened its gates to all-comers.

The fete was only for the élite who were up and about. The plebs on bedrest remained out of sight, enduring the hard labour of their incarceration. This was not Christmas: no concessions applied.

Ralph put on his best sports jacket and grey flannels, and polished his shoes. The whole atmosphere was charged with a sense of fun and escapism. 'You know what's first prize in the raffle, don't you?' Dai Check said, leering. 'A suck of Sister O'Neill's tits!' Even lewder possibilities were suggested. Llew the railwayman burst into song, something he'd learned in the male voice choir in Corwen.

The stalls and games were set up on the grass in front

of the Recreation Hall, 'the Rec'. Skittles, bagatelle, a bran tub, quoits, all innocent diversions that would have graced a vicarage. And darts! There'd been a dartboard at home, hung on the door to the 'cwtch' under the stairs. He decided to have a go. Sister Roberts was in charge of the stall, darkskinned, pretty as ever. 'Top score wins the prize! Three darts a go. You having a try, Ralph?' Her eyes twinkled.

'What's the prize?' he asked jauntily, thinking how poor a figure he'd cut with her soon after arriving in the San, when he'd felt all washed up.

'Wait and see,' she replied.

He took the darts, and as he did so their fingers touched—he could have sworn she'd contrived this deliberately, but her eyes shied away from his.

She stood demurely to one side of the dartboard: short, trim figure, crisp dark uniform, black-stockinged legs. Christ!

Carefully he weighed the darts in his hand, concentrating. He remembered playing darts with Bobby, the way his brother used to stand with hands clasped behind his back, waiting his turn.

I'm doing this for Bobby . . .

He took a deep breath, aimed carefully, and threw.

A double top!

Sister Roberts, startled, gave vent to a long 'Ooh' of admiration. He couldn't believe he'd done it—a double twenty first time, after being out of action so long!

One or two passers-by stopped to watch, as Ralph took aim again. The dart felt heavier than the first one, and his hand suddenly felt sweaty. Never mind, concentrate!

He let fly. Another twenty. Sixty in two darts!

Someone said, 'Aye aye, who's this, then?' Others stopped, so that they now had a thin line of spectators.

'Take your time now, Ralph,' said Sister Roberts, all admiration.

He tried to ignore her, and his unexpected audience. Should he go for the twenties again? Afraid he might hit one of the darts in the board out with a wild third throw, he went for the nineteens, down at the bottom of the board.

First he paused, running his fingers along the pointed end of the dart, simply to calm himself. He had to do it. He *had* to.

He aimed to put it anywhere in the nineteen bed but to his amazement it landed plum in the double. Thirty-eight with one dart! Ninety-eight altogether!

'Been practising, have you?' Sister Roberts gleamed. There were one or two handclaps, a cheer from someone, probably ironic. 'You're a dark horse, Ralph. Didn't know you'd had such a misspent youth.' She wrote the figures down. 'Highest by far yet, you little terror.' She smiled.

He wandered off, pumped up by exhilaration. Bobby would be proud of him! He saw his brother looking at him with his small, shy smile, hands clasped behind his back. 'Sense', Bobby said. It was a word that had held peculiar meaning for him, though no one knew what that was.

Suddenly, as if from nowhere, Ken Black appeared. Ralph almost failed to recognise him at first, for he was in brown corduroys, smart jacket and tie.

'What are you doing here?' Ralph asked stupidly.

'Same as you.'

'But—I didn't know you were up.'

'Should've come to see me more often then, shouldn't you?' said Ken, the lightness of his tone making this more of a jest than a reprimand. 'I'm on one and one now.'

'What block you on then?'

'J.'

'Why J?'

'Why not? Wouldn't want to be on the same one as you, would I?'

Although this was raillery, Ralph felt mortified. To have neglected his old friend so long! It was unforgiveable.

'Haven't met my father, have you?' Ken said. 'This is Ralph, Dad—you've heard all about him.'

'Indeed I have.' A tall man with square-cut glasses and kindly eyes clasped Ralph's hand. 'Only good things, don't worry,' he added, smiling.

Ralph, taken by surprise, mumbled something. He felt at a disadvantage, for there was something about Ken and his father, standing together, that made him feel inferior. It was partly the cut of their clothes, but something else: their self-assurance and easy, worldly manner.

'See you later then,' said Ralph, quickly escaping.

'Oh, don't go yet,' said Ken's father. 'Look around with us for a while.'

'I can't I'm sorry—I'm seeing someone,' Ralph lied.

'Oh yes?' Ken said archly. 'Who's that then?'

'Oh—nobody much,' Ralph said vaguely, plunging into the crowd.

He felt hot, embarrassed. He never knew what to say or do! Would he ever?

Next morning he wrote:

Dear Mam and Dad,

It was a special day here yesterday—the annual fete. There were all sorts of stalls and competitions and guess what—I won the darts prize! I had the highest score—98—the second highest was 85 so I won easily. I was given my prize by the matron—a packet of fags. I'm smoking one now as I write this— just like you Dad! . . .

He took another tentative puff. They'd made him feel queasy at first, but he was getting used to them now. He liked the look of the smoke as he blew it out, the slight dizziness in his head.

He did not think it strange that a place for consumptives should hand out cigarettes as a prize. In 1950, nobody did.

'Tuppeny-ha'penny stamp please,' said Ralph in the sanatorium post office.

George the Greek, behind the counter, gave him a cool look.

'Can't do. Run out.'

'You can't have!'

'You telling me? Come and look if you like. No tuppeny-ha'penny left. But I'll give you a tuppeny and a ha'penny instead if you like.'

'OK then. Just the same, isn't it?'

George impassively tore away an orange twopenny stamp and a halfpenny green one, both showing the well-groomed head of King George V1 with a crown poised over it.

Ralph slid a threepenny bit over the counter.

'Lot to say for yourself these days, Ralph,' he remarked, giving a halfpenny change. 'Comes of being a big boy on the grades, yes?'

'I don't know what you mean,' said Ralph, flushing.

'Not at all the boy you used to be, not at all. Wouldn't say boo to a goose before, would you?'

'Don't be silly.'

'Silly? Not me, boy. I don't go wandering off where I shouldn't be at night, no not George.' He shot Ralph a glance from beneath bushy eyebrows.

'I don't know what you mean,' said Ralph uncomfortably.

'No? Time you did then. Wouldn't get into trouble then, would you?'

'I'm not in any trouble.'

'Soon will be boy, if you go on taking walks at night. And what for I wonder. See pretty girl, maybe?' He reined in his voice. 'Take my advice, Ralph. You go and see my friend Des over in Hospital Block. He wants to see you, God knows why. Then I forget everything. OK?'

Ralph hurried out, his face crimson.

He knew he would have to visit Des.

11 Smoke Rings

Hospital Block smelt of rotting lungs and ravaged bodies and death just around the corner. It was the smell of the bug, concentrated and odious. No malaria-ridden swamp gave off more repellent a miasma. Every consumptive body, stale, sweaty and decaying, played a part in its making. Everyone who smelt it felt a sickening of the soul. The square white block, three storeys high, could well have borne the legend: 'Abandon hope all ye who enter here.'

Ralph took small, shallow breaths as he walked along the corridor. No dressing-gowned patients were to be seen here, popping into one another's wards for a chat. The thick, brooding silence was broken only by the sound of nurses swishing along the corridor, and the voice of the bug itself, torn from the throats of the diseased: sickly, damp coughs and the scraping up of vile mucus.

He stopped outside Des's single-bed cubicle: he could turn back, even now. But his visit, precipitated by George's blackmail, had grown into a challenge. Was he to turn away weakly yet again, as he had turned away at home from the dying Bobby, or face danger like a man? Even less excuse, now that he had the bug himself. Do lepers shun one another?

He pushed open the glass door; Des appeared to be asleep. He was facing away from Ralph, breathing deeply, painfully; there was something mechanical about it, and the back of his head seemed unnaturally small. Altogether he was diminished; the shape under the bedclothes was not that of the bullying, braggart Des of Block M. Ralph stood at the bedside indecisively; had he come to the wrong cubicle?

Des stirred, then coughed. And became aware of Ralph. His shit-coloured hair, dank and lifeless, pressed down on the pillow as he half-turned his head. Ralph, fearing what he might see, froze. Des slewed around heavily, stared at his visitor. 'Ralph,' he murmured weakly. 'Good old Ralphie.' He reached out an arm with stick-like wrist and clawing fingers. Repelled, Ralph drew back then checked himself. He took the claw hand in his, held it briefly, let go. The clammy touch of the vault was upon it; the body's corruption was but a breath away. 'I knew you'd come and see me,' said Des. 'Go on, sit down. Take a pew.' He made a large gesture, the lord of the manor intent on benevolence. Ralph hesitated, then sat on the wooden chair by Des's locker. He pulled it infinitesimally nearer the bed. 'How are you then, kiddo?' Des's voice, once thick and sticky with self-regard, was now hoarse; his eyes had lost their polar cruelty to become a thin and tentative blue.

'I'm OK thanks,' replied Ralph.

His own voice sounded strange to him, not least for its self-confidence. Moreover he was aware of looking at Des coolly, almost condescendingly.

'Good. What you on now then, you lucky bugger?' Des managed a twisted smile, as malformed as his depleted body.

'Grade Three.'

'Wish I was. Knew you'd do it, you bugger.'

'You will one day.'

Des grimaced.

'You're bound to,' said Ralph, feeling even as he said this a surge of superiority.

'I'm finished.'

'Don't be silly!'

'I am, Ralph. I tell you.' Des coughed, into his hand first, then his handkerchief. He stared at it, for flecks of blood. Ralph sat rigidly, willing himself not to move away or show any sign of fear.

'I'm fucked, mate. Truly fucked.' He raised himself on an elbow, wrenched up the pillows, lay back at a slightly higher angle than before. 'I was on blocks. They took them away. Weren't doing any good.' He coughed again. His fingers, raised to his mouth, looked waxen, transparent.

'What treatment they giving you?'

'Bugger-all. They've given up on me.'

'Don't be daft, mun!'

'I tell you.'

'What about an AP? They tried that?'

'Didn't take.'

'Oh. Well, there's always a PP. Phrenic.'

Des shook his head. The big word hung between them.

'Don't say thora,' said Des. 'They won't give me one.'

'Why not?'

'Don't know. Haven't asked.'

Des extended his arm again. 'Come nearer, you bugger. Not afraid of catching anything, are you? Not from your old buddy?'

'Course not.' He drew the chair closer, the corruption of Des's body ringing alarm bells inside him.

'Should think not.' Des's claw squeezed Ralph's arm, then retreated back under the bedclothes.

Des closed his eyes. 'You get the letters I sent you, Ralphie?'

'Yes,' Ralph replied, tensing at the use of the abusive 'Ralphie'.

'Thought you might have come sooner.'

'I couldn't.'

Des smiled faintly at the lie. 'Never mind. You're here now. Come to see your old mate, eh?' His eyes flicked open. Ralph tried to read what was in them. Surely Des hadn't forgotten the reality of Ward 8?

A reply died in Ralph's throat.

'Knew you would,' murmured Des.

He closed his eyes again. In the silence, the small sounds of Hospital Block reasserted themselves. A trolley tinkling along a corridor; a sudden snatch of high-pitched conversation between nurses, quickly silenced; the eternal scraping of throats and soft, mushy coughing.

'What happened to that bint?' asked Des suddenly. 'You seen her since?'

Ralph stiffened. 'Who's that?'

'You know who I mean, Ralphie boy.' Des's eyes were open: cold, brutal, unchanging.

A frozen lump lay in the pit of Ralph's stomach. He felt sickened, degraded.

'Had your fingers up her cunt yet? You should have.'

Ralph stood up shakily. Des's evil, probing eye was like that of a corpse resurrected.

Ralph opened the cubicle door. His whole body was trembling.

'Fuck off,' he said.

Des smiled triumphantly and made a V-sign with his claw.

His father wrote a jocular letter in his masculine, rightward-sloping hand. 'I'm sure your chalet was full of smoke, after winning that prize! Have one for me.' Ralph pictured him on the small chair by the fire, doing the football pools. Ten home wins; four aways; treble chance; flick-flick of the ash into the fire. Dad hardly ever smoked, and never drank. He lived a good, moral life.

Ralph felt the corruption of the sanatorium heavy upon him, within him. He was sickened by Des's duplicity and George the Greek's collaboration. He should have learned not to trust by now, but still he went on trusting. He was a moron, an imbecile.

What would he do when he got out? He knew, now, that he would not be here much longer. What work was he fit for? Nothing manual, but he would not want that anyway.

An office job, of some sort. A pen-pusher. An idler.

No, no idler. He wanted to be busy. And famous.

How could you be famous, working in an office?

Moodily he picked up a book, began reading it at random.

She was alone in the garden of Cherry Farm next Sunday morning. Slipping away early from his ham-

and-egg breakfast, he followed the path around the side of the house, afraid of bumping into her parents any moment.

She caught her breath when she saw him.

'You,' she said.

'Hope you don't mind. Sorry.'

'What for?'

'I don't know. Being here.'

'You shouldn't have.'

'I know.'

She glanced quickly at the back windows of the house.

'We can't stay here. Come along.'

She began to walk along a path between the vegetables beds.

He stood there, rooted.

'Come on, Ralph—quick!'

Hearing his name from her lips made his heart leap.

He followed her along the green path. Her trim ankle, above her brown shoe, was an exquisite work of art. The runner bean stems, climbing their poles, clustered more closely than those in the sanatorium grounds. There were raspberry canes, the fruits red and juicy as girls' lips. Everything here grew more abundantly.

The path ran the length of the garden to a wooden fence at the end. Beyond was a field where horses grazed, dipping their long brown heads into the grass. She turned to the right, facing him by the fence.

'You shouldn't have come round here. Why'd you do it?' she asked.

'I wanted to see you.'

'You mustn't.' She shook her head vigorously, some

strands of hair fanning out like the first spun threads of a web.

'I'm sorry. For what happened.'

'That's nothing. The point is—'

'What?'

'You know!' she cried helplessly.

'No I don't. Tell me.'

Her face was screwed up, as if subject to some insufferable tension.

'Please. Morwen.'

'Your illness!' she cried.

'What?'

'Don't you know? We're all scared of you here. Catching something.'

'But you let us come—you give us food!'

'That's all! Then you go away again.'

His own fear was in her. Fear was everywhere. It infected their entire beings.

She looked at him, pleading. 'It's not me, Ralph. It's them. They give you special knives and forks—did you know that? They put them away in a special drawer afterwards.'

'No,' he said slowly. 'I didn't know that.'

'It's awful. It's better they didn't have you here at all, than that.'

It sank slowly into him, the knowledge that his fear of Bobby had been only part of a greater fear, a swamp into which everyone and everything seemed to be sucked.

'I shouldn't have come here. I'm sorry.'

He turned to go back down the path.

'No! Not that way. They'll see you. Here.'

She beckoned him to follow her through tussocky grass to the top corner of the garden, where the fence petered out too soon, leaving a gap.

'You can get out through the field. There's a gate.'

Her eyes were fever-bright. He felt a hotness come out of her. He had to push past her to reach the gap. He was about to plunge through when she cried, 'Wait!'

She seemed about to say something then stopped. The rise and fall of her breast taunted him. Rebellion shot like a flame through him. He held her fiercely, running a hand through her hair. Then he let her go, almost throwing her from him.

'Ralph. Please.' Her hand went to her mouth, her eyes had a look he had never seen before.

He felt brutal, triumphant.

'Next Wednesday. Top of Haemmorrhage Hill. Eight o'clock.'

He turned brusquely, not looking back.

At night, in his chalet, he tried to blow smoke rings. There was a song on AFN:

> *If I had a cigarette*
> *I could watch the smoke rings curl*
> *But my joy would be complete*
> *If I only had a girl . . .*

But he did have a girl. Morwen.

He dragged the smoke down into his infected lungs. He could do so now without coughing.

The safest way out was round the back of Block N, then through a screen of trees. That took you to a short, steep slope where couch grass and wild flowers grew luxuriantly, like a small jungle patch.

He felt like crouching down or crawling up the slope, to avoid snipers' bullets.

Upright, walking so fast that he quickly got out of breath, he breasted the slope and clambered over the fence.

She wasn't yet in sight, but he didn't expect her to be.

He rested his arms on the top of a rusty gate, looking at the farmyard beyond. The soil was baked brittle-hard, and in the evening light everything had a dazed, languid look. Nothing stirred; the farm might have been abandoned. Then, suddenly, a whirl of gnats. He watched them as his heartbeat slowly steadied and his breathing became easier.

Her approach was so quiet that her appearance seemed sudden. His stomach lurched with the surprise of it.

'I didn't hear you coming,' he said.

'I'm sorry. Did I startle you?'

'Not really. You look nice.'

'Thank you.'

She sounded demure and looked it, in a cream-coloured blouse and light blue skirt. A brown mock-leather bag was slung over her right shoulder. He was surprised, and rather daunted, to see she was wearing a small crucifix on a gold chain. Was she sending out signals that she did not want to be touched?

Wordlessly, they began walking along the lane, away from the San. His heart was bumping again and he felt breathless, though not in the same way as before. They were slightly apart from each other, and the distance seemed unbridgeable. Speech too escaped them; he could think of nothing to say that would not sound stupid.

Suddenly she began talking. He was struck as much by the sound of her voice as by the things that she said. It was low-pitched, almost accentless; something else he had not properly taken in before.

'I shouldn't have told you that—about the knives and forks. It doesn't matter, not to me—honestly. I never think about it—catching anything, I mean. Nobody from the village gets it. You're all from away, aren't you? That proves it, doesn't it?'

She gave him a sideways, pleading look.

'Proves what?' he asked, confused.

'That you don't get it from being with people. Look at all the nurses you've got up there. And O'Rorke goes in every day with his papers.'

They walked on in silence.

'I didn't want to hurt your feelings,' she said. 'I could've killed myself after, when you'd gone.' She stopped. 'It's alright, isn't it?' Her eyes glinted.

'Of course it is. Don't worry, Morwen.'

He thought of kissing her but could not.

'Are you sure now?'

'Yes.'

She seemed defenceless and unapproachable; the crucifix held him in reproach for all he had set out to do with her that evening.

'The point is, Ralph,' she went on quietly, as they resumed walking, 'my parents must never know I've been out with you. Never.'

'That's alright. I never see them anyway.'

'But you might. When your mother comes to stay.'

'I don't think she's coming now. She hasn't been well.'

There had been a hint in his father's letter; nothing to worry about, son, but your mother's been a bit under the weather.

'What's wrong with her then?'

'Oh, nothing much I don't think. Probably her arthritis again.'

'This time of year? Does it come in the summer then?'

'Sometimes.' But he didn't know; he hardly knew how any of them were, because he had been away so long, and felt so distant from them all.

'Mam hasn't said anything about her not coming. Does she know, do you think?'

'I don't know,' he said irritably. 'I expect they'll be letting you know soon, anyway.'

'Yes, of course,' she said quickly. She added: 'I like your mother, Ralph.'

'Good.'

'She's very kind, and thoughtful. She even helps Mam with the washing up!'

'She would,' said Ralph, trying not to sound resentful. What did they know about his mother, any of them?

Morwen stole a glance at him. They had drawn nearer to each other, and suddenly both became aware of it.

He knew she wanted him to take her hand.

He was aware of her quiet breathing, aware of every pore in her body.

She began to say something then stopped.

He turned to her and kissed her roughly.

'Not like that Ralph,' she gasped. 'Please.'

'I'm sorry.'

She clung to him. She had on a perfume he had never smelt before.

Excitement raced through his body.

He kissed her, touching her breast through her clothes.

Their lips squirmed together, slack and exploring.

He began to unbutton her blouse.

'No!' she cried. 'Here.'

She took his hand, hurried him to a place where, ducking down, they got through the hedge.

He scarcely knew where they were. All he could see were her eyes dancing, her lips waiting.

They crushed down on to the grass. It smelt rank, as though the summer were turning sour.

He looked in amazement at her breasts; the shape so lovely, unexpected. He kissed her nipple but she shuddered. His hand cupped a breast as they kissed.

'No more now,' she whispered at last. 'No more now, please.'

He felt a relief that dismayed him.

She put her tongue out, as far as it would go, and he put the tip of his tongue against the tip of hers. She giggled.

'Go on now,' she said, sitting up. 'You've had enough for one night, Ralph Lloyd.'

'I've only just started,' he said, male-boasting.

She made the kind of sound that said, you devil, boosting his ego.

She straightened her bra and did her blouse up.

'Come on then,' she said. 'Time we were going home.'

He thought that night of the way the crucifix had lain in the sweet hollow between her breasts. Images of death and life, intermingled.

He dreamt of her and woke up hot and thrilling, the semen pumping onto his bedsheet.

12 Raspberry War

Picking raspberries. The soft red pulp stained his hands and made him think of Morwen's lips. He did little else but think of her, and of their next meeting the following Wednesday. She filled his being so completely that it seemed strange that it wasn't obvious to everyone. He felt exalted and irreparably changed.

It was the younger patients, about his own age or only a little older, who had been set to pick the raspberries. The long canes, twirled around by the stems and nippled by the bursting fruit, set them apart from all else. The boys worked quietly at first, indifferently dropping the fruit into their slatted baskets, but in time they became bored. Boredom made them boisterous. They began throwing the berries at each other, casually at first, but as reprisal became fiercer so did counter-attack. Soon a full-scale war was being waged, with accompanying whoops and cries and oaths, and the shirts of the warriors were splashed red with the blood of honour.

Dragged from his dreamy contemplation of Morwen, Ralph joined in exultantly. His heart pumped war-fever through his veins, he flung his ammunition joyously. So absorbed did he become that he was slow to notice the sudden hush, and his last badly-aimed sally squelched ludicrously into the grass in complete silence.

'When you've finished, Mr Lloyd, would you please come and see me?' said Jock. 'The rest of you get on with your work. Mr Smythe will be coming down to supervise you, since you insist on behaving like children.'

He turned and coolly walked away, his head resting squatly on his broad shoulders. From the rear he was even more the pugnacious prize-fighter, his hard fists clenching and unclenching as he strode from the battlefield.

Everyone was staring at Ralph. He realised he was trembling. Shakily he picked up his toppled basket, turned again to the rows of canes.

A hand gripped his arm. 'Christ, you're for it now. You'll get the high jump, most likely.' The wild, strained face of a boy everyone called Lucy, a play on his surname rather than a comment on his manhood.

'Don't be dumb, Lucy.' The calm voice of Bryn Davies, beanpole-thin, reassuring. 'We were all in it. Jock could see that.'

'Why'd he ask Ralph to go and see him then? You better be getting up there fast, boy.' Lucy pushed his glasses up, blinked through the strong lenses.

'He caught him in the act, didn't he? He had to do something,' Bryn said.

'He caught us all. Why din't he have us all up there, eh? Tell me that. He's going to make an example of you kid, throw you out probably.'

Dissident voices threw a lifebelt to Ralph. He looked around hopefully, seeking consolation.

'I'll tell you what's going to happen, boys bach,' said Ray Jenkins, thin fair hair combed flat to his scalp, voice reedy and complacent. 'You're going to get a right ticking-off, and that's all. He can't overlook it, but you were the last to be caught. You see if I'm right or not.' He looked around unctuously, a minister of religion in the making.

The boys looked uneasily at one another, shamefaced for getting Ralph into trouble.

'I don't know about that. You can never tell with Jock. He's a bastard.' The quiet voice of Elwyn Humphries, at twenty-two the oldest of the chain-gang. 'Tell you what, though. If he does anything to Ralph we all go on strike. Agreed?' His eyes swept the company. No one spoke. 'Well, come on then,' appealed Elwyn. 'Do you agree or don't you, you yellow-livered bastards?'

Loud cries of acclaim reassured him. 'Well then, that's it, Ralph!' he cried triumphantly. 'If he victimises you we're out on strike—all of us!'

Ralph's eyes shone. Never had he been a hero. A phrase glittered suddenly in his brain: Working-class martyr. That's what he was—a working-class martyr!

'Now you get along up there.' Elwyn pumped his hand, then shepherded him between the tall rows. 'We'll do bugger-all till you come back and tell us what happened. Will we, lads?' he cried, throwing his voice high. 'We'll refuse to do any more picking even when Smythe comes along, stupid cunt. *If* he comes, that is.'

At the far end of the rows, Elwyn clapped Ralph on the back. 'Off you go then, son. Remember, we're all rooting for you.'

'Thanks, pal.'

Ralph set off jauntily, but as he neared Jock's office— in a mock-gothic building still called The Mansion—his spirits fell. He could be sent home. Expelled. To have a relapse, probably.

All his fear of dying returned.

The Mansion, once the home of a squire who had

owned all these acres, housed the admin staff of the San and Jock's private quarters. Here too he had the office where his forced labourers came every Monday to be given their allotted tasks. It was set apart from the prison-like huts of the patients, not only in distance but in height, for it stood at the top of the grounds fringed by a brooding copse of conifers. Even in summer it exuded a gloomy air, its depressing effect on the spirits helping to damp down any spirit of rebellion that might spark briefly in the chests of these consumptives.

Ralph automatically wiped his feet on the rubber mat at the entrance and stepped into the chill, intimidating hall. The bronze bust of a long-dead squire thrust out from the gloom below the massive, polished stairway. He tapped a door to his right inscribed 'Medical Superintendent'.

'Enter.'

Surprisingly, Jock was alone: he had expected Sister McGaw to be there, breathing her disapproval over everything.

'Come along in, Ralph,' said Jock. 'Sit down here, laddie.' He waved a hand benevolently: he was even smiling.

Ralph first felt shock, then relief, then an enormous sense of gratitude. He had been forgiven! He must have been!

'Thank you,' he said, making his way to the vacant chair in front of Jock's broad, mahogany desk.

'There's someone to see you,' said Jock, glancing to his left.

Confused, Ralph did not properly take in his words. He was almost sitting down before he saw his brother

Joe standing by a window, almost concealed by the antique screen that stood beside it.

'Joe! What are you doing here?'

'I'll leave you to it, Mr Lloyd,' said Jock gravely to Joe, who nodded and advanced grimly on Ralph.

'What is it? What's wrong?'

Joe gripped his hand, and put his free left hand steadyingly on Ralph's forearm.

'I've got some bad news, I'm afraid,' Joe said. 'About Dad.'

Ralph felt a quick, shaming sense of relief, that it was not Mam who had died.

'He had a heart attack two days ago. He died yesterday.'

'Oh.'

'We didn't want to worry you. There was nothing you could do.'

'No.'

He ought to feel something but could not. He didn't know what to say.

'I thought I'd come along and tell you. Myself,' said Joe haltingly. Tears brimmed in his blue, honest eyes. He was twelve years older than Ralph, always the big brother.

'Yes. Thanks.' Ralph felt he should be consoling him; Joe had always been closer to Dad.

'Mam OK?' he asked.

Joe nodded, gulped. 'We thought you'd like to come home—for the funeral. Dr Maxwell said it's alright.'

Ralph looked around wildly. Jock had gone. The empty chair left Ralph feeling naked.

'I don't think I can,' said Ralph. 'I mean—'

He didn't really know what he meant. All the words, themselves, the room, seemed to be spinning round in a muddle. He put his hand on the table, to steady himself.

'Here,' said Joe. 'Sit down. I'll get you some water.'

Ralph sprawled in the chair, thinking: I won't be seeing Morwen. Wednesday's gone. For ever. Dad's dead. Dad's dead.

He thought of Dad's words in his last letter: 'I'm sure your chalet was full of smoke . . . Have one for me.'

Have one for me . . .

The poignancy of the words sank in. But still he could feel no emotion.

The train rumbled on, through the green wasteland of Mid Wales. Ralph looked indifferently through the window at sights he had not seen for two years. The engine whistled now and then, a thin and oddly hoarse sound, as if it suffered catarrh in its chimney; smuts whirled in from time to time through its wide-open window. Ralph, indoctrinated with the fresh-air regime of the San, had insisted on its being so. He sat in a corner seat, Joe opposite.

Joe had changed; he was more solemn than hitherto, and not simply because of the death in the family. Ralph had noticed it during his occasional visits, a drawing-in of his spirits, a reluctance to laugh as he used to. His whole face seemed heavier, as if it were prematurely settling into middle age. He was barely turned thirty, yet he had the manner of someone much older. Ralph wondered if he had been disappointed in love yet again. He could not read his eyes because they were turned away from him, even in conversation. They were hidden too behind thick-lensed glasses with posh frames, not NHS glasses at all.

It was all so different from what he had imagined it would be, this journey home. He had never believed it possible that he would make it only on parole instead of as a fully-discharged patient. And Dad dying! It was incredible. He forced himself to think of the times Dad had taken him out when he was small, his chubby legs dangling either side of Dad's head as he sat high on his shoulders. The nursery rhymes Dad had sung:

> *Gee ceffyl bach, yn cario ni'n dau,*
> *Dros y mynydd i hela cnau,*
> *Dŵr yn yr afon, a'r cerrig yn slic,*
> *Cwympon ni'n dau. Wel, dyna chi dric!*

He tried to squeeze out a tear, but his eyes were dry.

Joe sat reading the *Daily Mail*, hardly looking up.

The telegraph wires dipped, soared up to the next pole, dipped down again.

The train stammered through points, then found a new rhythm.

It would be rest hour in the San, the boys on grades lying fully-clothed on their beds.

Des would be getting weaker and weaker.

Morwen would be in school, eating her lunchtime sandwiches probably.

Dad's d-d-dead said the train, Dad's d-d-dead dead-dead-dead dead-dead-dead.

Smuts flew on to his hair. He let them stay there, grey with foreboding.

'Oh, bach.' His mother launched herself at him, arms opened wide. He flinched from them but she held him close, her cool cheek pressed to his.

He looked down at the frayed green tablecloth, so familiar yet utterly foreign.

She let him go and he moved away thankfully, picking up his suitcase and saying, 'Where've you put me? I'll take this up.'

'I've put you in with Joe. Don't mind, do you? I'm in your old room with Gwen. Your Dad's in the front room of—' She choked on the words. He hurried upstairs.

The house was much smaller than he remembered. The stairs were poky, so narrow that his case bumped against the wall as he climbed.

The front bedroom door was shut tight. He went into Joe's room.

Somehow Mam had found space for a single bed as well as Joe's double. Ralph dumped his case on the single bed in relief; he had feared she might have put him in the double with Joe. There had been a time when he'd have shared, without question. But he was older now, and used to sleeping on his own.

He tip-toed past the front bedroom on his way down again, as if Dad might hear him and call.

Bobby had died in there before him: a room of death in a house of strangers.

After the funeral he tried to shut out the chatter of relations and neighbours talking about nothing in loud voices. He ate a sandwich or two but did not feel hungry.

'Cup of tea, Ralph? Duw, there's healthy you're

142

looking. Done you the world of good, that place. Remember how thin he was?' Mrs Prendergast, brown china teapot in hand, appealed to Mrs Evans. 'Could hardly see him, poor dab. Look at him now!' Tea spurted into his cup, dark as Sunday.

Ralph smiled faintly, tried to be pleasant. He longed for the peace of the San, the company of people he knew.

He went into the garden. It was scrubby, ill-cared-for. He thought of the neat vegetable plots in the San, the springy lawns, the clipped hedges. And of the brief Raspberry War which had ended so abruptly.

Jock had said nothing about it. The Old Man now seemed human.

'Come out for a bit of peace? Can't say I blame you.'

Gwen, smiling beside him. The eldest in the family, always in control.

'Sorry I haven't been to see you much lately. Been a bit awkward, with this new job. I was thinking of coming down next month, if you're still there that is. That alright?'

'Course. Come when you like.'

'You're looking really fit. They'll be letting you out soon, I take it?'

'I haven't got a clue.' He longed for a cigarette, but didn't want Gwen to know he was smoking. It would only end up with a lecture, as usual.

'What are you going to do then, after?'

The note of deliberate unconcern alerted him.

'After what?'

'After you come home, of course! You're going back to school, I take it?'

'Don't be daft. I couldn't do that.'

'Why not? You're only eighteen. You're young yet.'

He said nothing.

'You really ought to, you know.' The old note of imperiousness was there. 'You ought to do your Matric, go on to university.'

He wanted to say: Fuck university!

'You'll be sorry if you don't, Ralph. Believe me.'

'Give it a rest, Gwen,' he said, and went back indoors.

'You can stay longer if you like, bach,' said his mother. 'Dr Maxwell won't mind, I know. He told Joe, let him stay as long as he likes. You're practically cured now, aren't you? Maybe you won't have to go back at all,' she said hopefully.

'Don't be silly, Mam. I'm not discharged yet. You know that.'

'Well, stay for the weekend anyway. You can have some nice walks on the prom. You'd like that, wouldn't you?'

'I'm going back tomorrow, Mam. I don't want to take any chances.'

His mother sighed, gripped her handkerchief tight.

'I'll be awful lonely,' she said. 'Without you and Gwen.'

'You'll still have Joe, Mam.'

'Oh, I know that but—I never stop thinking of Bobby. And now your father.' She dabbed her eyes.

Ralph stared down at his hands.

She sighed again, and went to the scullery.

Joe went with him to the station. There had been a tearful farewell to his mother.

'Well, old chap,' said Joe, jovial now he was leaving. 'Hope you'll be back again soon—for good.'

'Yes.'

'I'll try to get down there soon, before the autumn. But you may be home by then anyway, won't you?'

'No, I don't think so.'

'Oh, won't you?' Joe seemed about to say something else, but changed his mind.

The guard blew a quick peep-peep on his whistle.

Through the open window they exchanged final courtesies.

As the train drew away, Joe lifted a hand.

Ralph sat back in the empty compartment. He felt a huge sense of relief.

13 Freedom

Sunday afternoon. Visitors. They debouched off creamy-white Swan coaches from Swansea, scarlet Western Welsh buses from Cardiff and the Rhondda, stumpy little Austins and Morrises rattling along self-importantly, huge, hearse-like taxis bumbling up from the railway station. They brought cakes and fags and chocolate saved up out of their ration, local rags and weekly mags and endless bonhomie.

'Soon be home now, boy. Duw, you're looking better!'

'What they got you doing now then, wass? Fit as a flea you are now I reckon!'

'Auntie May sends her love look, and these beautiful Welsh cakes—delicious!'

He was glad to feel he played no part in their world, glad to sink down fully-clothed on his bed in Block G and clap on his headphones, a free man in the safety of the San.

Stan Kenton's band was on AFN, brassy and brazen and big-chested, the trumpets climbing to cacophonous heights in 'The Peanut Vendor.' Ralph, isolated amid the din only he could hear, felt he was someone with no past and no future. The abrupt death of his father, something in which there appeared to be no logic, was like the last word written in a book he had put aside. The old life was gone now, as completely as if a light had been switched off. There was no going back to that redbrick house by the river. He didn't belong there; and, in his heart, he knew he would never belong anywhere again.

He was aware of her before he actually saw her. He turned his head then wrenched off the headphones, sitting up in confusion.

'Morwen! How long have you been there? I'm sorry.'

'I've only just come, don't worry. What are you listening to?'

'Oh, nothing. Come on in. I'm sorry—there's only this chair—'

He stood up in his stockinged feet, pulling the chair round for her to sit on.

'Ralph, I'm alright. Please.'

She seemed as cool as he was hot, befuddled.

'I didn't know you were coming. Did you say?'

'No—course not,' she said, puzzled. 'Ralph, I'm so sorry—about your father.'

'Oh—yes—'

'I didn't know if you were back. I thought you might be staying.'

'No.'

'Was it awful?'

'Pretty bad.'

He saw now that she felt as awful as he did, only disguising it better.

'You got my letter OK then?' he asked.

'Yes. Thanks for letting me know.'

'Had to, didn't I? Or you'd have been waiting for nothing.'

She blushed a deep crimson.

'Like a walk?' he asked, inspired.

'Yes—that'd be nice.'

'Just a mo' then.'

He bent to put on his shoes, his back to her now. When he turned he half expected her to be gone but she still stood there, just inside the doorway.

'Right then. Let's go.'

They turned left outside the block, by unspoken agreement, towards the drive that would take them out of the San. This was respectable enough; within the laws of the institution, for a patient on grades with a visitor on a Sunday afternoon.

Some of the boys he knew best saw him, giving him meaningful glances he did his best to ignore.

At the top of the drive she hesitated. 'Could we go somewhere else, do you think?'

A scene switched on in his head: Haemorrhage Hill, a gap in the hedge, the tip of one tongue touching the tip of another, a mock-gold crucifix lying in the cleft between two white breasts.

'We'll go on a round if you like. That's what we call it,' he added.

It was the walk he had taken so many times before: one circuit of the San in the morning, one in the afternoon, two in the morning, two in the afternoon, one and one, two and two, three and three ad infinitum.

The clouds were high, stretched-out, presaging rain. The hills looked exhausted, sucked dry. Mynydd Troed alone was aloof, uncaring, neither enhanced nor diminished by the strain of the summer.

They had not walked far when she said, 'Can we sit down somewhere? I'm tired.'

'There's a seat just round the corner—not far.'

It was a simple wooden bench in which generations of consumptives had carved their initials.

She sat heavily and in silence, looking down at her hands. He could not bridge the gap between them.

'Had he been ill long—your father?'

'No. He had a heart attack—very sudden.'

'I don't know what I'd do,' she said at last. 'If it happened to me.'

He wanted to apologise for not seeing her, but how could he?

'What did you do then?' he asked. 'Last Wednesday night?'

'Nothing much. Just stayed in doing my homework.'

It was the day he had gone into the front bedroom on his own, pulled back the white sheet and looked his last on his father's tight, waxen face in the coffin.

'When shall I see you then—' he began.

Her gesture stopped him. 'I can't, Ralph. I'm sorry.'

'Why not?'

'I just can't, that's all.'

His face hardened. 'They've told you not to, haven't they?'

She looked at him pleadingly.

'How did they find out? You didn't tell them, did you?'

'No—of course not!'

'Well then. How'd they know?'

'They opened your letter.' She saw his face. 'I couldn't help it, Ralph—it wasn't my fault!'

'Do they always open your letters?'

'I don't get any! That's the point!'

She wiped away her tears with her hand impatiently.

'I should have known,' he said despairingly. 'I shouldn't have bothered to write.'

'I'm glad you did.' She blew her nose. 'I'm so sorry for you, Ralph—really I am.'

'There's no need. I'm alright.'

She looked at his tense, hurt face.

'I couldn't go on seeing you anyway,' she said quietly.

'Why not?'

He saw the answer in her eyes.

'You mean you've . . .' He couldn't believe it, after what had happened between them. 'No!' he gasped.

'I'm sorry, Ralph.'

'Who is he then?'

'A boy I know. I've known him ages.'

'What's his name?'

'Gerwyn.'

'*Gerwyn*,' he said contemptuously.

'Don't *say* it like that!' she flared.

'I'll say it any way I like—you can't stop me!'

He stood up angrily, staring across the roofs of the prison blocks to the hills beyond Mynydd Troed.

'Country bumpkin, I suppose—is he?'

'Yes. Just like me.'

'Don't be stupid.'

She saw his face and was frightened.

'Don't you touch me—don't you dare!'

'I wouldn't dream of it.'

She stood up shakily. 'I'm going home now, Ralph.'

'Go then.'

She began walking away.

He remembered her coming to see him the first time; the way he'd kept her waiting in the doorway.

He wanted to call after her but could not.

He thought she might look back but she did not.

She turned the bend in the pathway.

Also by Herbert Williams

Poetry:
Too Wet for the Devil
The Dinosaurs
A Lethal Kind of Love
The Trophy
Ghost Country
Looking Through Time

Fiction:
The Stars in their Courses (short stories)
Stories of King Arthur (for children)

Biography:
John Cowper Powys
Davies the Ocean: Railway King and Coal Tycoon

Other non-fiction:
Voices of Wales
Come Out Wherever You Are
Stage Coaches in Wales
Railways in Wales
Battles in Wales
The Pembrokeshire Coast National Park